ON THE EDG

The Gilbert
by Cat Cahill

Chapter One

Cañon City, Colorado Territory - 1876

Something was wrong.

James Wright rose from the desk, his paperwork forgotten. It was a scent—roast beef, if he wasn't mistaken—that infiltrated the sheriff's office in Cañon City.

He glanced down at his pocket watch. 7:00. Well past time to lock the door and head upstairs to his supper obligation. He smiled at the thought. As one of two regular sheriff's deputies in town, he'd been the supper guest of the sheriff and his new wife more than once over the past few months. The taste of the food didn't always live up to the promise of its scent, but James enjoyed it nonetheless. After all, it was much better than whatever he could scare up himself, and the conversation was far improved from eating alone at the little restaurant across from the dry goods store.

James pulled the shades and locked the door before making his way to the stairs in the rear of the building. The cells behind the stairs were mercifully empty for the first time in weeks. He climbed the narrow steps to the small living quarters on the second floor where he paused to knock—but the door flew open before his knuckles met the wood.

"James!" Mrs. Young stood in the doorway, a large wooden spoon in her hand. "You're just in time." She left the door open as she disappeared through the room into the kitchen.

Three plates of meat, potatoes, and carrots sat on the table already, steam curling up from each one. Ben Young, the county sheriff and James's boss, stood from his seat. "I was about to fetch you from downstairs." He pushed a chair out, and James took it gratefully.

"Lost track of time," James replied. His stomach rumbled, and it took all of his willpower not to grab the fork next to his plate. Finally, Mrs. Young reappeared, a gravy boat in her hands.

James waited until Mrs. Young had said a prayer, and then gathered up his fork as fast as possible. He closed his eyes at the first bite. It was heavenly—and worlds different from the first time the Youngs had invited him to supper. A satisfied sound escaped his lips.

"I take it that means you're enjoying the food?" Mrs. Young asked.

"It's perfect," he replied. "Thank you for inviting me, Mrs. Young."

She set her fork down. "For the love of all good things, James, you're to call me Penny."

James nodded uncomfortably as Ben laughed. Mrs. Young—Penny, he supposed—never stood much on ceremony.

"Anyway, it's much improved, isn't it?" Penny smiled at her husband and James. "The girls would hardly believe me if I told them I could cook something without scorching it or boiling all the taste out of it."

"Do you see your friends often?" James asked, reaching for his glass of water. Penny had worked as a Gilbert Girl—a waitress—at the hotel in Crest Stone, south of Cañon City, before she married Ben.

"Not recently. But they'll come up for church services now that the snow has melted. Although I suppose it won't be long before Crest Stone has its own church."

"When that happens, you'll have to take the train down for a visit." Ben smiled at his wife.

A few months ago, James never would've imagined Ben as a married man. And now here he was, easily settled into a new sort of life. It was a life James couldn't imagine for himself, as appealing as it seemed at times. He had plans for what he wanted to achieve as a lawman, and a woman would only serve to distract him.

"The town's growing so quickly, I fear they may need someone like you there all the time," Penny said to Ben.

"They'll elect a marshal once they're organized enough to consider such a thing," Ben replied. He sat back in his chair, finished with his meal, and fixed his gaze on James. "But it has been weighing on my mind since that train robbery last month. And now with all the newcomers arriving to help build, I've a mind to send someone down there to help keep the peace. James, you'd be the best choice for that. You want to go?"

James paused in the middle of chewing his meat. This was the first Ben had mentioned of such an idea. He swallowed and lifted the napkin to his lips before responding. "You wouldn't need me here?" He forced himself to sound neutral to the idea, when in reality, he wanted to jump at the opportunity. He'd been a deputy here for going on two years; he'd saved up enough experience that he was more than ready to strike out on his own, be the sheriff or town marshal somewhere. Maybe this was that opportunity, coming to land in his lap without him even needing to lift a finger.

"I've got Harry, and if we need, I can always deputize Eli Jennings again. Heaven knows he's always asking," Ben said.

Penny landed a stare on her husband that would've melted a lesser man. Ben cleared his throat and apologized to her for his choice of words, but with a smile so James couldn't tell if he was entirely sorry or simply appeasing his wife.

"In that case," James said, "I'm happy to go as soon as possible."

"I must admit I'm a bit jealous that you're going to see the town grow. Just don't fall in love with any of the Gilbert Girls." Penny aimed a mischievous grin at him.

James laughed, even as he could feel his neck go red. "I won't have time for anything such as that."

"Ben didn't either." Penny laid a hand on her husband's arm as she gave James an appraising look. "You could use a good woman."

James shoved a last piece of meat into his mouth. That was the last thing he needed right now.

Ben shook his head. "Leave the man be," he said before turning his attention to James again. "I'll wire the hotel so they'll know to expect you."

They spent the remainder of the meal discussing the growth of the town with lively interjections from Penny. When he left, James took a moment in the office downstairs to gather his thoughts before stepping out into the night to find his way home. This opportunity was exactly the sort for which he'd been waiting. Recently, he'd thought he might need to go seeking it out, but he'd been loath to leave a good position here in Cañon City for the unknown.

Now it appeared he might be headed toward what he really wanted. Taking this work in Crest Stone was the logical next step. Were his uncle still alive, he would've slapped James on the back in congratulations and then told him not to mess this up.

James smiled at the thought as he pulled on his coat. Uncle Mark had understood him in a way his own parents never could. He was the reason James had left the dull security of the family farm in Kansas for the uncertainty of life in the Colorado Territory. If James could be half the man his uncle was, he'd feel like he'd accomplished something good in his life.

He'd go to Crest Stone and do the man's memory proud. And maybe by this time next year, he'd be Marshal Wright.

Chapter Two

Crest Stone, Colorado Territory

Edie Dutton snuggled deeper into her coat as she closed the book she'd borrowed from Mrs. McFarland's small library. The hotel manager's wife, who served as the bookkeeper, was still kind enough to lend Edie books when she delivered dessert to Mrs. McFarland each evening. Although Edie didn't know why, she was grateful. In fact, most everyone at the hotel was friendly and kind to her, which was puzzling. She thought on it from time to time, but hadn't yet settled on *why* exactly. After all, it wasn't most folks who would continue to take kindly to a young woman who stole from their place of business, even if she had been blackmailed. As much as she could figure, it was simple Christian charity.

She laid the book on the little garden table and scanned the trees that lined Silver Creek, which ran the length of the valley. It was early May, and spring was evident all around even though the mountains that rose high above the creek were still a snow-covered white, almost blinding in the afternoon sun.

Edie sighed. It wasn't often she felt entirely contented, but when she did, she wanted to seize the moment in the hopes it might last forever.

"Oh, thank goodness!" a harried voice sounded from behind her, interrupting the fleeting peace.

Edie turned and spotted Adelaide, who at sixteen was one of the youngest Gilbert Girls at the hotel. Edie herself was only a couple of years older, but her own life at sixteen had been so different from the one Adelaide was living.

"I *must* go to the mercantile, and Mrs. Ruby says I can't go alone given all those new men who have arrived, but everyone else is either working or otherwise occupied. *Please*, will you come with me?" Adelaide held up her hands as if in prayer, her big eyes sparkling in the sun.

Edie might have laughed if she was given to such reactions, but instead she smiled. "You've found me at a good time. I've only just finished my book, and I'm not scheduled to work this evening."

Adelaide clapped her hands together. "Oh, thank you! I'm all ready. I've left my coat in the kitchen."

Edie gathered her book and followed Adelaide inside. "I must return this to Mrs. McFarland, and then we can go."

"I'll join you. What were you reading?" Adelaide finished shrugging into her coat and reached for the book. "*Herbs and Medicinal Plants of the Colorado Territory*. You do choose books that would put me right to sleep. I much prefer novels about dashing dukes and their ladies or pirates on the high seas. It's a pity Mrs. McFarland doesn't have any books like those."

She handed the book back to Edie, who clutched it to her chest as she pictured Mrs. McFarland curled up with a dime novel about a pirate. A rare giggle came to her lips and almost escaped. The contentment she'd felt earlier must be going to her head to conjure up such images. "I enjoy learning about plants and trees." She paused a moment, wondering if she should share more, then plunged ahead. "I hope that as soon as the weather is warmer, I'll be allowed to plant a small garden."

"Why, Edie Dutton," Adelaide said as they made their way through the busy hotel lobby, "I had no idea you were a farm girl."

Edie's fingers tightened around the book. "I'm not. I mean, my mother tended a garden and we had a few horses and goats and chickens, but . . . no, my family aren't farmers." Adelaide didn't need to know most of those horses weren't really theirs, or that the goats and chickens were necessary since they couldn't often go into town to purchase milk or eggs or meat, just like she didn't need to know anything else about Edie's previous life in Kansas. No one did.

Mrs. McFarland was not in her office in the north wing of the hotel, so Edie slipped the slim volume into the pocket of her skirt. She'd come back later. She didn't dare try the knob to see if the room was unlocked, not after what had happened earlier this winter when that horrible Mr. Adkins had forced her to steal from the hotel to repay what he thought her pa owed him, or else have her darkest secret made public. It was a wonder Mr. McFarland had allowed her to remain employed as a Gilbert Girl and hadn't put her on the next train back to Kansas.

Not that she would ever return home.

The girls returned to the expansive lobby, which bustled with guests, hotel employees, and men who had arrived in the valley since the snows had melted to begin building the town. Adelaide waved to Dora and Emma, two former Gilbert Girls, who sat near the fire. Emma's hands rested on her growing stomach, while Dora held sheets of paper in her lap. Edie smiled at them. She was always hesitant to presume anyone was her friend, and although Dora and Emma had never been anything but nice to her, she feared they might see through her somehow. Particularly Dora, who had discovered Edie was the one stealing from the hotel. Yet Dora had remained ever kind, even after Mr. Adkins had held them both at gunpoint in the hotel's stables.

"Emma tells me her baby isn't to be born until late June, although it looks to me as if it could arrive any day now," Adelaide whispered as they pushed open one of the large doors and stepped back out into the sunlight. "I cannot imagine ever having children. Can you?"

Adelaide was forever making broad pronouncements such as this, and it amused Edie to no end. "Oh, I believe you'll have a whole passel of children. Seven, at least. Perhaps ten," she teased.

"Ten!" Adelaide pressed a hand to her heart. "My mother had only my brother and myself, and she remarked often about how trying it was."

"Oh, it isn't so bad. Having so many children in a family, I mean. I have five brothers." Edie clamped her mouth shut. She never shared details about her family. What had possessed her to do so now?

Adelaide shuddered. "One brother was plenty for me. Having another four to boss me around sounds like a nightmare come to life."

Edie searched in vain for a new direction of conversation. The last thing she wished to discuss was Adelaide's sheriff brother. She scanned the horizon from where they'd begun to walk down the hill toward the depot and the burgeoning town. "Oh, look," she said weakly, "what do you suppose that will be?"

"Which one?" Adelaide asked. No fewer than five new buildings were under construction on both sides of the railroad tracks.

"The one by the smithy shop." Edie chose a partially constructed building at random.

"A livery, perhaps? It would make sense to have it next to the blacksmith's."

"It's awfully small to be a livery." Edie was truly curious now. In fact, the entire new town made her curious. It was a miraculous thing to see something arise from wilderness like this. When she'd first arrived, this place had felt so big and *empty*. Being from Kansas, she was used to wide open spaces, but to see an entire town emerge from such a place was an entirely new experience. It was fascinating to watch, but deep down inside, it made her nervous. More buildings meant more people, and she'd already had the misfortune to be identified by Mr. Adkins. Who else might arrive here if it turned into a proper town?

Adelaide shot a grin at her. "Then let's go find out." The younger girl was nearly to the depot before Edie caught up with her. Edie picked her way across the railroad tracks and the mud lying on each side, her breath coming quickly from the unexpected sprint down the hill.

"Pardon me," Adelaide was already calling out to the men working on the mystery building.

A warm flush crept up into Edie's cheeks. Adelaide was overly exuberant at times, which could be endearing, or—such as now—could be far too forward.

"Adelaide!" Edie whispered loudly as she closed the steps between them. But Adelaide paid her no mind.

"My friend and I are wondering what this building might be once it is finished. Could you tell us?" Adelaide smiled at the young man who'd answered her call, and he went a bit red.

"It'll be the land office, miss," he said, rubbing the back of his neck. "The railroad bought up all this land when it laid tracks."

Edie let her eyes wander the partially built structure. It was hard to imagine these pieces of wood would turn into a building one could use.

"Thank you, sir. You're doing a wonderful job," Adelaide said, as if she were in charge of the building. She tucked her arm around Edie's, and they started toward the mercantile and general store, which was only just south of the to-be-built land office.

"Good afternoon, miss!" the man called a half-moment too late. Edie knew if she looked back, she'd find the poor man watching Adelaide walk away.

But as for Adelaide, the man and the land office were already forgotten. She steered them around some mud and said, "Oh, I hope Caroline has some lace handkerchiefs. She told me she would order some. My handkerchiefs are a frightful mess, and I must have at least one new one before we go to services in Cañon City on Sunday."

"Can you not edge a square of cotton if you're in such need?" All of Edie's handkerchiefs were plain cotton, and they served their purpose just fine.

"I suppose, if I don't care to catch the eye of any fine gentlemen who happen to be at services, too."

"And a lace-edged handkerchief will do just that?" Edie could hardly imagine any man even taking notice of a lady's handkerchief, much less whether or not the thing had lace. Her brothers were lucky enough to even remember to carry them.

"Of course! If you hold it just so, as if you have a cough, it will frame your eyes very nicely." Adelaide pretended to hold a handkerchief to her face.

Edie bit her lip. That was the most preposterous thing she'd ever heard, and she was about to tell Adelaide exactly that and remind her that as a Gilbert Girl she was forbidden from being courted anyway, but the girl had already pushed open the door and was halfway inside before Edie could speak.

Caroline Drexel, a former Gilbert Girl who ran the store with her husband, greeted them from behind the counter. While Adelaide nattered on about lace handkerchiefs, Edie perused the store's shelves. The Drexels kept many items in stock for the hotel employees and train passengers. Edie could only imagine how their business would grow as the town did.

She paused by a shelf holding an array of bottles, both small and large. The bottles were a rainbow of colors, and all bore labels proclaiming such things as *Ivers Cure-All—For Lungs, Throat, and Stomach* and *Dr. Smith's Tincture for General Health and Well-Being*. Edie thought back over the herbs and plants she'd grown at home and the new ones she'd read about in Mrs. McFarland's book. She tried to imagine herself brewing up some medicinal concoction so incredible, people would demand it be bottled and sold in stores such as this. *Miss Dutton's Elixir of Life*. The name brought a smile to Edie's face—until she realized one tiny detail was incorrect.

Dutton was not her surname.

Chapter Three

James shaded his eyes from the sunlight as he took in the buildings under construction. There were four—no, five—in various stages right now, with the foundations of two more looking as if they'd begin to take shape over the next week. He hadn't had the opportunity to visit Crest Stone before. Ben had spent a lot of time down here, particularly last fall when Royal Hagan's gang had taken his sister, but James had remained in Cañon City to keep the peace there while Harry and Eli had accompanied Ben.

It was a pleasant enough spot, this burgeoning little town in the valley. Nestled near the foot of the Sangre de Cristos to the west with the smaller Wet Mountains several miles to the east, it was picturesque. Or at least, it would be, once the construction was completed. Right now, it was a muddy mess.

James had stopped at the hotel first to introduce himself to the proprietor. The man, one McFarland, had treated him to lunch, for which James was grateful, and had offered him a small room on the second floor of the hotel. After settling into his room, James decided to meet as many of the folks working on the new buildings as possible. He'd met Mr. Thomason, the depot clerk, who he learned also served as the postmaster and the telegraph operator. And now he'd come to the first building under construction, a small place next to an existing blacksmith's shop.

Clanging sounded from the smithy's, and James paused, pressing his eyes shut. The familiar ache pressed against his forehead as if it were fighting to find a way out. It had been threatening ever since he'd left the hotel, but he'd ignored it. He didn't know how long it would be before it would render him utterly useless—it varied every time. He gritted his teeth, and for probably the millionth time in his life, wished for any other burden to bear than these headaches. The pain subsided to a dull reminder. The respite would be brief, he knew that, but he'd take advantage of the time he had before he'd need to pull the curtains in his hotel room and lie in bed.

"Afternoon," a voice said.

James's eyes flew open. The last thing he needed here was to look weak. He pasted a smile on his face, held out a hand, and introduced himself. "Afternoon. James Wright. Fremont County sheriff's deputy."

The man narrowed his eyes for a half-moment before smiling in return, removing his work glove, and shaking James's hand. The look didn't bother James. He'd seen it time and again. It was most folks' natural reaction to learning his occupation as they immediately wondered what he wanted with them.

"Stephen Bauer. Good to meet you. Is there trouble?"

"No, not at all. I'm down here to keep that from happening. I just got into town and thought I'd meet folks." He took in the wooden frame behind Bauer. "Will this be your establishment?"

The man laughed. "Wish it were. This'll be the land office for the Colorado & New Mexico. They bought up all this land when they laid the tracks, and now I suppose they'll make money off selling it to people."

James resisted pressing his fingers to his forehead as the pain pinged against his skull. Instead, he grabbed hold of the nearest post and ground his nails into it. "You work for the railroad?"

Bauer nodded. "Not directly, though. You want Monroe Hartley. The railroad hired him to oversee construction of this place. Same as some other interests in town. I think he's down that way." Bauer pointed south along the tracks, toward more new construction.

"Good to meet you," James said. If he weren't pressed for time with this ridiculous infirmity, he'd have taken a few minutes to meet the other men working on the land office. But for now, he needed to move on and find this Hartley, and perhaps meet the proprietor of the general store and mercantile. The others would have to wait until tomorrow.

He pressed on through the gritty mud that had formed between the buildings and the railroad tracks. The mercantile door opened as he walked around a particularly wide puddle, and out stepped a figure in a simple calico dress. An unbuttoned coat covered her shoulders, and a plain yellow hat adorned her head. She made a cheerful impression among the men and mud and wooden frames, so much so that he smiled in spite of the pain that had triggered again inside his skull.

The woman had only just stepped away from the mercantile when James knew she was in trouble.

"Miss, wait!" he shouted, but it was too late.

One misplaced foot slid away from her, and before James could act, she'd landed on her hands and knees in the mud.

He arrived at her side a split second after she fell and offered her a hand. "Are you all right?"

"I . . ." Her voice trailed off as she lifted a mud-covered, gloved hand, and stared at it for a moment. Instead of taking his hand with her own, she offered him an elbow.

James took her elbow and—awkwardly—helped her rise from the mud. Upon standing, she looked down at herself and winced. "Thank you," she said so quietly he almost didn't hear her.

"You're welcome," he replied. He wished he had something to offer her. A towel perhaps, or . . . "I'll run into the mercantile and see if they don't have something you can use to clean off your dress."

"No, please, don't." She looked at him now, her face tinged pink beneath the brim of her yellow bonnet and a pair of thin, silver-framed spectacles. She was only a few years younger than James himself, perhaps eighteen or nineteen, and so slight it seemed she might blow away in the breeze if the mud weren't heavy enough to hold her down. He felt like a giant next to her.

He paused, caught halfway between taking a step toward the mercantile and staring at the endearing blush on her cheeks. "Might I at least offer to—"

"Oh, no. Oh, no, no, no, no, no." The girl leaned over and extracted something from the mud.

James tilted his head as she shook some of the mess off a book. It appeared to be a slim, leather-bound volume, and he couldn't imagine why she'd be carrying such a thing about town.

"It must've fallen from my pocket," she murmured as she tried to wipe off the remaining mud. It did no good at all, considering her gloves were both muddy. Her movements grew more frantic. She was certainly more concerned with the state of the book than the state of her clothing, as most women would be.

Extracting a handkerchief from his pocket, James reached for the book. She held on to it for a moment, as if she didn't trust him with it, and then relinquished it when he held up the handkerchief. "Follow me."

She trailed behind him as he made his way to the rear of the mercantile where a small yard opened to a barn. James squatted down among the sagebrush and the remaining brown winter grasses mixed with the bright green of the new spring shoots. He found a particularly dense piece of sage and ran the covers and spine of the book against it to remove the excess mud before taking the handkerchief to it.

The woman peeled off her muddy gloves and watched quietly, until he handed the book back. It wasn't perfectly clean, but as good as he could get it. "If you run a damp cloth over it when you return, that should take care of what remains."

She pressed the book to her chest. "Thank you. You didn't have to ruin your handkerchief for me."

James grinned. "You looked as if you were about to lose your dearest friend. *Herbs and Plants of the Colorado Territory*, if I remember correctly." He didn't add that the title had taken him by surprise. It seemed a weighty subject for a girl so slight.

"It's borrowed. I'd hate to return it in such a state." Her voice was soft, and something about it conjured images of an inviting hearth and a plate full of delicious food.

James shook the bizarre thoughts from his head. "I'm happy to escort you home," he said in his most professional voice.

Her cheeks went pink again, and all he could think about was how she still seemed a ray of sunshine in that yellow hat, even though she was now half-covered in brown, sandy mud.

"Thank you, but that isn't necessary. I must wait for my friend, and besides, as you can see, this town is very small."

He laughed, and she gave him a tentative smile. "Are you employed at the hotel, Miss . . . ?"

"Dutton," she supplied. "And yes. I'm with the Gilbert Company."

"I'm James Wright. I had a mighty good dinner there earlier. It's a fine establishment."

She lifted her chin, and it was easy to see the pride that flickered across her face. "I'm happy you enjoyed it." She paused a moment, and then after seemingly deliberating asked, "Did you only just arrive in town?"

Something about her curiosity—concerning him—made him go warm inside. "I did. I'm a deputy to the county sheriff. With all the new people coming in and out of Crest Stone, I'm here to ensure it all goes without trouble."

Miss Dutton's eyes widened, and James felt pleased with himself. He'd impressed her. Perhaps she'd like to hear of one of his adventures, but before he could settle on one story, the headache pressed ferociously against his eyes, so hard his stomach rolled. He turned away for a moment, trying to get hold of himself and willing the pain to dissipate for just a little longer. He'd offer to walk both her and her friend back to the hotel. It was self-serving—not only would he get to spend a bit longer with her, but he'd also be that much closer to collapsing into his dark room for a few hours.

"Miss Dutton . . ." he began as he turned back toward her.

But she wasn't there.

He strode to the front of the mercantile and searched left and right until he finally spotted her, the hem of her coat covered with mud, coppery brown hair glinting in the sun, and book clutched in her hand. She fairly ran across the tracks a little ways down, making her way toward the hotel.

James blinked after her. Had he done something? Perhaps she'd thought it rude when he turned away. These blasted headaches. He clenched his hands as the pain made itself known again. What he wouldn't give to rid himself of them entirely.

But it was for the best. He had no time for such distractions. And now, if he wanted to salvage any part of the rest of this day, he needed to lie down. Some lawman he was, requiring a nap in a dark room in the middle of the afternoon.

And so he put one foot in front of the other, willing the ache to fade just long enough to get back to his room, and watching a fascinating, muddy figure move quickly up the hill to the hotel.

If she wasn't within sight, he'd have wondered if he'd met a ghost.

Chapter Four

Edie slumped against her shut door, trying to catch her breath. It wasn't the first time in her life that she'd found herself running, but certainly the first time while wearing a dress weighed down with drying mud. She'd come in the back door near the laundry room and hotel offices, and had been lucky to only pass a bellboy and another Gilbert Girl—who'd offered to help her with her dress. Edie had politely declined. She wanted to be alone for a while to ponder what had just happened.

She crept gingerly across the floor to set the book on the vanity table she shared with her roommate Beatrice, hoping not to make such a mess she'd need to scrub the floor later. Then she set about removing her soiled coat, gloves, dress, and shoes. She wasn't certain if any of it was salvageable, but she'd give it her best try.

Luckily, Beatrice had forgotten—again—to empty the pitcher and bowl from that morning. As Edie scrubbed splattered mud from her face and wrists, she realized she'd left Adelaide alone at the mercantile. She'd need to ensure Adelaide had returned safely—and hadn't wandered off to enjoy conversation with whomever caught her eye—after she cleaned herself up and changed into fresh clothing.

Edie tried to keep her mind on Adelaide and not think of the man she'd just met, but it was impossible. He must think her half-witted with the way she'd run off without a word. Although he probably already did before that, considering she could barely string together two words without blushing. Just remembering the way she acted sent the warmth flaming up into her cheeks again.

It was such an odd reaction. She'd spent her life around her brothers and various other men who'd worked with her family. It wasn't as if she was uncomfortable around men. In fact, the easiest part of her work at the hotel was making conversation with the frequent solo male guests in the dining room. She spoke to them like she'd spoken to her brothers, and they always seemed at ease around her. She was quite adept at shutting down any flirting that had come her way, and never feared the rougher-looking cowboys or railroadmen, the way some of the other, more sheltered girls did.

So what was it about this Mr. Wright? Or was it Deputy Wright? She didn't even know the correct way to address the man, never mind why her ability to think seemingly disappeared around him. It reminded her of when she was about fifteen, and her brother Ty's friend had come to stay with them for several weeks. He was maybe nineteen, with an easy smile and hair that was as black as a raven's feathers. Every time he caught her eye, Edie felt as if she'd forgotten how to breathe, much less make words. And so she'd avoided him completely, feigning illness to skip supper and keeping to parts of the house where he wasn't.

She paused, the ivory cloth against her cheek, and stared at the whitewashed wall as the realization dawned upon her. Deputy Wright might not have raven-black locks, but his dark blond hair curled over his collar in a way that made him seem too busy to bother with cutting it, and while his smile didn't seem as easy as that other young man's, it was true and intriguing. Not to mention his green eyes, the hard line of his jaw, and the confident way in which he carried himself . . .

Edie dropped the washcloth into the basin. She found him handsome, and that was why she'd stumbled over her words. It wasn't why she'd run—that had more to do with his line of work—but it was certainly why she hadn't enjoyed his company with more grace.

Her mind went immediately to the possibility of seeing him again. It was more than likely, considering he had to be staying at this hotel. She could avoid him, the way she had with Ty's friend, but . . . She gripped the edge of the basin as she realized she didn't want to. She *wanted* to see him again. Wanted to try to speak as she normally did. Wanted to take note of *his* reaction to seeing her again.

But even as the thoughts cascaded through her mind, Edie knew better. It was a dangerous sort of thinking. She couldn't feel that way about any man, particularly one in his line of work. When she left Kansas, she concluded she'd never be married. And while sometimes that knowledge gave her a twinge of sadness, for the most part she was fine with it. After all, she was good at being alone. She enjoyed being a Gilbert Girl, and so long as she had a garden to tend as the weather warmed and books to read and company in the other girls, she could be happy.

Not to mention there was always the possibility that someone might find her again. The idea of another Mr. Adkins arriving made her stomach tie itself into knots so tight no sailor could ever undo them. And with the town growing as fast as it was, that likelihood grew stronger each day. There wasn't much she could do, other than keep to her false last name and be very aware of all who arrived. Ever since the incident with Mr. Adkins, she'd paid close attention to the guests' conversations she overheard in the dining room and lobby, the girls' gossip in the employees' parlor, and the goings-on among all the hotel staff in the kitchen. And when she ventured down to the tracks where the building was happening, she kept her eyes open for any familiar faces. Mr. Adkins's arrival had happened entirely by chance—he hadn't known she was here until after he accepted the position as one of the hotel's stable hands—but who was to say something similar wouldn't happen again?

And worse, what if Mr. Adkins had told others she was here? He'd been sent to the territorial prison in Cañon City, while she was still here, free as a butterfly in a field of flowers. The only reason he hadn't spread her secret immediately after his arrest was that she'd told him at their last meeting that she'd already written her father about him.

It kept Edie up some nights. If Mr. Adkins ever suspected she'd told him a fib—and that her father wasn't even aware she was in the Colorado Territory, much less that she'd been at the mercy of Mr. Adkins's threats—there would be nothing to stop him from telling anyone he happened to pen a letter to from within the prison walls about her whereabouts.

She shivered and stepped over her soiled clothing to the wardrobe, resolving to set such worrisome thoughts aside for now. Thanks to her waitressing salary—and having no family to send it to—she'd been able to purchase a few ready-made dresses in Cañon City. None of them were particularly fancy, but they were more than she'd had when she arrived. She selected a pretty blue gingham that reminded her of the spring sky.

With this dress on, her hair freshly brushed and repinned, and a smile upon her face, Edie thought she looked more like the girl who'd been offered and accepted the position of Gilbert Girl than the scared young woman who'd snuck out of her family's home late at night with nothing but a small carpetbag, a few borrowed bills, a forged letter of reference, and a desire to leave Kansas as quickly as possible.

She'd worked hard to become Edie Dutton, and she intended to remain Edie Dutton for the rest of her days. And that meant she needed to avoid Deputy Wright at all costs, even if he was the most handsome man who'd ever arrived in Crest Stone. And she certainly had to forget the way he'd smiled at her as he'd taken in her face, even when the rest of her was covered in mud . . .

The very thought made her heart trip a little faster.

Edie frowned at herself in the small mirror she and Beatrice kept on the vanity table. Feelings like that toward any man would cost her the position she'd worked so hard for. Courting was forbidden for Gilbert Girls, and she only need look at her friends who'd since married to see the truth in that. But worse, feelings like that toward a lawman could prove even more dangerous.

She set down the mirror and sighed.

It was impossible to outrun the shadow of a father who was the most wanted man in the state of Kansas.

Chapter Five

When he awoke several hours later, James held his breath until he was certain the pain in his head was gone. As he moved from sitting to standing and felt no ache at all, he was able to breathe again. Outside his window, the sun had disappeared behind the mountains, but it couldn't be too late since it hadn't yet sent a spray of oranges, pinks, and yellows across the sky.

James's stomach grumbled, reminding him it was now time for supper. He smoothed his rumpled clothing, found his hat, and let himself out into the hallway. At the second-floor landing, he could tell he'd awoken just in time. People streamed through the lobby toward the dining room. The six o'clock from Santa Fe must have only just arrived.

He moved quickly down the stairs to join them, but stopped in his tracks when a figure in a vibrant blue and white dress emerged from the hallway that branched off the lobby near the dining-room doors. That bright penny-colored hair shone in the lamplight, and she smiled as she listened to the chatter of her companion, a young blonde girl who was speaking nonstop. The copper-haired girl was Miss Dutton, who somehow looked just as radiant covered in mud as she did now in a clean dress.

His feet took two steps toward her before he realized what he was doing. The very second she looked up, he took a hard turn to the right, into the room that housed the lunch counter. Despite its name, the lunch counter was open for supper, too. It served the men who preferred eating quickly and without the fuss of the dining room. Considering he'd only just arrived in town, James hadn't been in this room before, but he now took a seat at the counter between a ragged-looking man and a railroadman whose clothes bore the evidence of soot.

Turning, he snuck a glance back out the door, but Miss Dutton and her companion were long gone. He didn't know why he'd avoided her in that way.

Disappointment wafted through him, which was utterly ridiculous. He was in Crest Stone for one reason only—to maintain order as the town grew. And nothing about that required him to befriend a beautiful woman who carried books about plants in her pockets and who disappeared midway through a conversation. It was good he'd avoided her just now. Distractions would not serve him well.

"Good evening, gentlemen." A woman dressed in the same gray and white as the waitresses in the dining room stood poised before him. "I'm Miss Barnett, and I trust you're doing well this evening." It wasn't phrased as a question, and so James—along with the men on either side of him—nodded in agreement. Miss Barnett went on to tell them of the menu options that evening, and after placing an order for roast beef and potatoes, James decided to get on with his work and meet the men on either side of him. The more people he knew here, the better he'd be able to do his job. He'd learned that from his uncle years ago.

He turned to the scruffy-looking man to his right. "Name's James Wright. I just arrived in town today." He'd also learned early on that people were more comfortable if he spoke with them some before telling them what he did for a living. His badge was hidden under the jacket he hadn't yet removed.

The man eyed him for a split second before, James assumed, deciding he was worth spending words on. "Caleb Johnson. Haven't been here long myself. Hartley hired me on to build."

Hartley. That was the second time in a day James had heard that name. He'd meant to find the man earlier, before the blasted headache had made him take refuge in his room. "Certainly is a lot of work going on here. I met a few men working on the land office earlier."

"My crew is working on the bank." Johnson nodded at the waitress, who was filling their mugs with steaming coffee.

"A bank?" James furrowed his brow, trying to discern the point of having a bank when there were so few people in town. Although he supposed it would come in handy down the road, as the town grew.

"According to Hartley, the fellow who's opening it hopes to get business from the hotel and the railroad. There's also the miners east of here, but between you and me, they're broke the second they get paid." Johnson stirred milk from the little pitcher the waitress left on the counter into his coffee.

James picked up his own mug and blew on it before taking a sip. This was good information to know. If the hotel didn't have a nearby bank where it kept its funds, it must be keeping them on the premises. They probably had a safe, but it still sounded like a dangerous proposition. He made a note to speak with McFarland again tomorrow. He also needed to ride out to the mining outfit at the base of the Wet Mountains at some point and make himself known to whatever lawmen that company had likely hired on to keep peace among the miners.

"Once that land office opens, they'll be doing a brisk business. Not to mention the other businesses that'll be built soon," James said.

The man nodded. "More work here than up in Denver right now. The moment I heard someone was hiring on men to come down here and work, I signed up."

"You're out of Denver?" James asked. Uncle Mark had told him years ago that people were more than happy to talk about themselves if you set them up with questions. He'd taken that to heart; knowing about people was crucial in his line of work.

"Not born there—came from Wisconsin when I was young—but spent most of my life there. My pa was a railroadman." The man sipped his coffee. "How about you? Passing through?"

James shook his head. "I'm a deputy to the sheriff up in Cañon City. Just down here to see everything goes well as the town grows." He watched the man out of the corner of his eye, an old practice that had alerted him on more than one occasion when a man had something to hide. But Johnson merely nodded and drank more of his coffee.

But James only stared at his steaming mug, remembering the moment Miss Dutton had chosen to run. Was it a reaction to learning his profession? It was impossible to know for certain, considering he'd been turned away from her with that blamed headache when she'd taken off.

Their meals arrived at that moment, and the scent of roast beef, mashed potatoes, and hot greens made it difficult not to begin shoving the food into his mouth as fast as humanly possible. James shrugged off his jacket and began to eat.

After a few moments, Miss Barnett arrived across the counter, a rag in one hand. "How do you find the roast?"

James swallowed. "It's excellent, thank you."

"I'm glad you're enjoying it, Sheriff. I'll be sure to tell the chef. He'll be quite pleased."

James glanced down at his badge. "Deputy. Send him my regards." Just as Miss Barnett was about to move on to the railroadman next to him, James was seized with a wild idea. "I met another Gilbert Girl in the town today."

"Oh?" She raised her eyebrows. "Mrs. Ruby doesn't allow us to walk alone past the tracks now that there are so many more men here."

He hadn't meant to get Miss Dutton into any trouble—only to learn more about her. "She had come from the general store, so I'm certain her companion was inside."

Seemingly appeased, Miss Barnett nodded.

"I didn't catch her name," he lied, "but I'm hoping you might be able to help me. She was small, reddish-brown hair, spectacles . . . ." He didn't add that her hair shone like a coin, or how she smiled when she'd seen how he'd salvaged her book, or that he couldn't stop thinking of her.

"That would be Miss Dutton," the waitress said.

He'd hoped for a given name, but he supposed that would have to wait. "She had an interesting manner of speaking. Do you know where she comes from?" Another slight lie, as Miss Dutton didn't have any sort of accent that he'd noticed.

"Kansas, I believe."

He tried not to show surprise. "I also hail from Kansas."

Miss Barnett nodded and glanced down the counter at her other customers. He was keeping her from her work. Only one more question, and perhaps that would satisfy him. "I wonder why she would come all the way here."

Miss Barnett gave a small laugh. "Oh, we all have different reasons. Some girls only want an adventure, others need to provide for their families, and some want to escape their circumstances."

Which one was Miss Dutton? He pondered the possibilities as Miss Barnett narrowed her eyes just slightly at him.

"Forgive me if I overstep," she said, "but I feel I should inform you that in order to work for the Gilbert Company, we all sign contracts promising that we will not allow ourselves to be courted. To break that rule is to lose one's position."

Immediate discomfort made James straighten in his seat. He didn't know what had given Miss Barnett the impression that he wanted to court Miss Dutton, of all things. "I assure you that my questions are merely professional. It's my job to get to know people."

She nodded her head, then gave him a slight, knowing smile. "You asked me nothing about myself." And with that, she was moving down the counter to converse with her other customers.

He stared after her, her remark echoing in his ears. He'd meant his questions to be professional, but were they? James returned to his food, chewing thoughtfully until laughter sounded from outside the door behind him. He instinctively turned, and upon seeing an older woman escorted by her husband, felt a strange hollow sort of sensation inside.

It only took him a few seconds to puzzle out why—he'd hoped the source of the laughter was Miss Dutton.

He sighed and speared the last of the meat with his fork as Mrs. Young's words danced through his head again. *Just don't fall in love with any of the Gilbert Girls.* He'd laughed at the ridiculous idea when she'd said it. But now, it was easy to see how such a thing could happen.

What was wrong with him? He'd barely been in town a day, and he was already mooning over a woman. James pushed his plate aside. He'd only met Miss Dutton once, and she'd run away from him. Besides, he knew better. His uncle had allowed himself to be taken with a woman, and that had been his downfall. James refused to fall into the same trap.

"Pardon me, sir, are you Deputy Wright?"

James turned in his seat to see a boy of about fourteen or so, scrawny with a hat too big for his head, holding a folded piece of paper. "I am. And you are . . .?"

"Christopher Rennet, sir. I assist Mr. Thomason at the depot with the telegraph machine. There's a message for you." The boy held out the neatly folded bit of paper.

James stood and fished for a coin in his pocket, held it out to the boy, and took the telegram. Finished with his supper, he paid the waitress and returned to the privacy of his room. The message was most likely from Ben, and paying the cost of a telegram meant it was something important.

James took a deep breath and unfolded the paper.

Chapter Six

E die deftly carried two plates of steaming hot breakfast food through the dining room until she reached the small table in the corner. Two friendly faces glanced up at her when she arrived.

"This looks delicious," Dora said as Edie set the plate of ham and eggs in front of her. "Thank you."

"You should sit," Emma said, nodding at a nearby empty chair. "Surely Mrs. Ruby won't mind."

Edie smiled as Dora giggled. They all knew Mrs. Ruby certainly *would* mind. Edie could sit when she finished the breakfast shift, but not before.

When Edie returned after checking on her other tables, Dora had finished but Emma had eaten only a small amount of her food.

"Did it taste all right?" Edie asked. Emma needed to eat, considering she was expecting a baby in less than two months.

"Oh, it was wonderful, but I can only seem to eat food in small amounts these days. I'm ravenous, and then promptly stuffed, all day long." She looked longingly at the nearly full plate as she rested her hands on her stomach.

Edie collected their plates. "Adelaide and I went to visit Caroline's store yesterday. I can hardly believe all of those new buildings. Mr. Hartley must be busy." Mr. Hartley had also built the hotel, before Edie arrived, and fallen in love with Emma. Edie had heard the story from the other girls time and again, but one fact had stuck in her mind—Emma had lost her position at the hotel when she and her now-husband were found out.

"He is, but I'm happy for him," Emma said. "Oh! I haven't told you girls yet. He's planning to build us a small home in town."

Dora clasped a hand over her mouth. "Does that mean you'll be staying here?"

"What about his building work?" Edie asked, holding the dirty plates. Emma's husband traveled often to build all sorts of places. They'd only just returned to Crest Stone, and Edie was under the impression they'd move on again once he finished his work here.

"He promised me at least a year," Emma said. "We have the baby coming, and he'll have plenty of work to keep him busy here for that long. By that time, I'm sure we'll both be ready to see somewhere new." She looked at her friend across the table. "Will Mr. Gilbert be building a home for the two of you in town?"

"I'm not certain yet." Dora glanced down at her hands. "He seems eager to find work away from the hotel, but he doesn't know what he'd like to do instead. He has a head for business, so he could do anything, really."

"He could help you in your venture," Emma said, a teasing note to her voice.

Edie grinned as Dora shook her head, smiling. It amused them all to no end to picture Dora's husband— the son of the man who owned the hotel—assisting with his wife's soon-to-be mail-order bride idea.

"I must be patient. He'll figure it out," Dora said. She reached over and laid a hand on Edie's arm. "How are you doing?"

It didn't matter that they saw each other frequently; Dora always asked after Edie. It was touching, but also made Edie want to slink away as it never failed to bring her wrongs to mind. It was her fault that Dora had found herself held at gunpoint last December, her fault the hotel had almost needed to close, and her fault that Mr. Gilbert had needed to come here at all. Although, she supposed, that last part hadn't worked out so badly, considering he'd fallen in love with Dora and married her.

"I'm well, thank you. Although I nearly ruined one of Mrs. McFarland's books yesterday. It's a wonder—" She stopped midsentence as she noticed neither Dora nor Emma were looking at her. Instead, their attention had moved behind her. Edie turned to see what had captured her friends' interest—and nearly dropped the plates she held.

It was Mr. Wright. Deputy Wright, she reminded herself. He stood just inside the dining-room door, and was motioning to her. Edie clutched the plates even harder. It couldn't be *her* he wanted. She'd barely even met the man, and she certainly didn't know him well enough to allow him to seek her out in a busy dining room while she was working. She turned back toward the table and forced herself to breathe normally.

"Edie? I believe that gentleman is wanting to speak with you," Dora said gently.

"If he'd like to eat, he can find a seat like every other guest," she said, her voice pinched.

Dora and Emma exchanged glances. "Do you know him?" Emma asked.

Edie squeezed her eyes shut for a moment. "Yes," she finally said. "Barely."

"Then perhaps you should do him the courtesy of finding out what he needs. Despite the garish manner in which he's summoned you." Emma gave her a little push on the arm.

Other customers were beginning to notice him now. It wouldn't be long before Mrs. Ruby came bustling out to discover what he needed. Edie decided speaking with him was a safer choice than letting him continue to draw attention. She drew in a deep breath and moved as quickly as she could toward the deputy.

"May I be of assistance?" she asked, trying to keep the tremor from her voice. She hated that she couldn't treat him as she treated every other man she met. Why couldn't she simply force herself to act normally around him?

"I'd like to speak with you in private," he said, his hat in his hands and looking every inch the assured lawman. Petrified or not, Edie's mouth went dry at the very sight of him. Surely this man had a sweetheart back in Cañon City. He was far too handsome not to.

"I'm afraid that's impossible," she whispered. "We cannot be—"

"I doubt your superior would question you aiding the law. Even Gilbert Girls must be good citizens, correct?" He held her gaze with those green eyes, and Edie found herself nodding in spite of her better judgment.

She'd steer him toward a corner in the lobby. That would afford privacy and yet not be scandalous. Taking the lead and praying no one would gossip about her to Mrs. Ruby, Edie slid through the dining-room doors, Deputy Wright on her heels. She stopped by a large window that overlooked a cozy seating area and one of the massive stone fireplaces that flanked each end of the wide lobby. It was early yet, and so the chairs were empty. But they were in full view of the few people in the lobby so as not to cause scandal.

The deputy glanced about the room, seemingly taking in every person present. "This isn't what I had in mind."

Edie went to cross her arms, only to find she still held the dirty plates. "No one will overhear you, if that's what you fear."

He was silent for a moment, his gaze retracing the entire room before landing back on her. Edie had the strangest sensation that he could see every little thing she was hiding. Perhaps that was what he wanted to speak to her about. Maybe he'd somehow discovered her true identity. The thought made her shiver.

"Are you cold?" he asked.

"No." She straightened her shoulders and held his gaze. "Please, do tell me why you need so desperately to speak with me."

"I've received a telegram." He reached into a pocket and retrieved a folded piece of paper.

Edie stared at the ivory rectangle. What could be in that message? Was it Mr. Adkins, throwing caution to the wind? Or was it someone else—someone who knew who her family was? Someone who knew her real name. She wanted to drop the dishes and crumple into the nearest chair. Everything she'd built here for herself would be whisked away in a moment. What would she do then?

"There's been word that some men wanted in Kansas have moved into the Territory," he began. "We don't know if it's the Beaumont gang or the Fletchers or someone else."

Edie thought she might be sick. She pressed the plates into her stomach. He knew. He had to. Why else would he be telling her this information? She doubted any of the other girls at the hotel were familiar with those names.

"The sightings have been far east of here, so there is no need to worry." His eyes crinkled as he looked her up and down. "Please, sit. You look about to faint."

Edie couldn't move. It was as if the soles of her shoes had grown into the polished wooden floor. She leaned against the back of the nearest wing chair, hoping that might help keep her upright.

"Forgive me," he said. "I forgot to mention that Miss Barnett at the lunch counter informed me you were from Kansas. I also grew up there. Being from the area, I knew you would be familiar with those names and that you might have connections back home who may have apprised you of the comings and goings of these outlaws. I know they've terrorized all corners of the state for years. It seems they choose one area to work for a time before moving on."

"I . . ." Edie couldn't think of what to say. It was the last thing she'd ever thought she'd need to speak on without having to defend herself. "I'm aware of them."

"Yes . . ." Deputy Wright trailed off, apparently waiting for more.

Of course, everyone who lived in Kansas knew of the Fletchers and the Beaumonts. Never working together, the state had seemed plenty big enough for both gangs to continue stealing what they chose and evading capture since before Edie could remember. They remained on the fringes of the cities, preferring instead the desolate plains and lawless towns—close enough to be a menace, but far enough away that the city folk couldn't be bothered to round up Pinkertons or federal marshals or anyone else for very long to put an end to both gangs. And so they'd continued, year after year, doing as they pleased and staying out of each other's territory. The few times they'd clashed had been violent, but quick.

Everyone knew of the Fletchers and the Beaumonts.

Especially Edie.

But the deputy didn't know that. At least, it *appeared* he didn't know that.

"Deputy Wright," she finally said. "I have no family left in Kansas, and very few friends. I don't correspond with anyone I knew there. I doubt I can be much help."

He turned his hat in his hands, those sharp green eyes still on her. "I'm sorry. That must be hard. I apologize if I've made you uncomfortable."

"It's quite all right. I'm well past any grief over my family." That was certainly the truth, whether or not her previous statement about her family was also.

"May I ask that you keep this news to yourself? As I said, this area is in no danger, and I hate for folks to think it might be."

"You have my word."

"Thank you, Miss Dutton. I don't suppose you know of any other hotel employees who might also be from Kansas?"

Edie shook her head. "I don't." She paused for a moment, her gaze drawn to the sunlight streaming in the east-facing window. It lit up the valley, making every bit of sage, each railroad tie, and each partially built business look as if it had been touched by heaven itself. It was a marvelous sight, and Edie would never grow tired of it. It was a small miracle that she was even here, safe from her uncertain life back in Kansas. "Please, Deputy Wright, do you think they'll come here?" She turned back in time to see his face go soft, concern darkening his eyes.

"I can't say for certain, but I doubt they will. They've never left Kansas before, and I doubt they'll remain over the state line very long."

Edie bit down on her lip and said the shortest, most fervent silent prayer she ever had. If God would only keep her safe here, she'd do anything.

The deputy pressed the heel of his hand to his forehead and grimaced.

"Are you quite all right?" Edie asked.

"Fine. Thank you." He dropped his hand, although his face had paled considerably. "It's only a pain in my head. I've gotten them since I was young."

"Headaches," Edie said thoughtfully. "But you get them frequently?"

"Sometimes." He furrowed his brow. "I must get back to my room." And with that, he turned on his heel and was gone toward the stairs, leaving Edie clutching two dirty dishes, a fear that had lodged in the pit of her stomach, and an idea sprung from the book on local herbs and plants she'd just finished.

Chapter Seven

When James awoke hours later, he opened his door to find a small canvas bag tied with a string. A folded note sat under the bag. Curious, he took both bag and note back into the room.

Steep a spoonful in boiling water to make a tea when you feel the pains coming on. The tea should soothe the ache.

The note was unsigned, but James suspected he knew who it was from. He ignored the heat that seemed to crawl through him at that thought, and opened the small bag to peer inside. Thick silvery green leaves, torn into tiny pieces and mixed with darker green dried leaves, looked back at him. The scent was pleasant, almost minty. Having little knowledge of plants, he had no idea what the herbs might be, but he was willing to try anything. He set the bag and note aside and let himself out, trying in vain not to think of a certain lovely woman combing the lush area near the creek for the right plants to help him.

James spent the remainder of the day wandering the various building sites and meeting more people. The sky had just begun to darken when he met up with Mr. Johnson and the crew working on the bank. The men came from all over—Denver, mining towns, places back East, Texas. James tried to remember each name. It would get easier with time, but for now he'd just have to stumble past remembering the best he could.

He was bidding the men good night when someone shouted his name from a distance.

"Deputy Wright!"

James squinted into the shadowy evening to see two young women racing toward him. One was taller with curls escaping from under her white cap, while the other was smaller, her hair neatly pinned up and her spectacles perched on her nose. Both Miss Barnett and Miss Dutton wore their gray and white work dresses and aprons and no coats, despite the cold.

They stopped just short of him, completely out of breath. Miss Dutton placed a hand to her chest, and her pretty face was flushed with exertion.

"Good evening, ladies," he said for lack of anything else to say.

"Deputy Wright, you must come quickly," Miss Barnett finally said. "There is a disruption at the hotel."

"A disruption?" He began walking along the tracks, the ladies at his side.

"Two men were arguing at the lunch counter, and it erupted into a fight. It spilled out into the lobby and now there are at least four men involved. Mr. Mc-Farland and some of the desk clerks and bellboys were trying to pull them apart, but I fear you may need to become involved." Miss Dutton lifted her skirts to walk even faster.

James wasted no time. He ran across the tracks and up the hill to the hotel, the women on his heels. When he threw open the hotel door, the ex-citement still continued. Stunned guests, railroadmen and builders, waitresses, and maids circled the melee in the middle of the room. James forced his way through the crowd, only to find himself in the middle of a fight worthy of Mur-ray's Saloon in Cañon City. McFarland, in a suit and tie, had pinned one of the fighters to the floor, while various other hotel employees worked to separate the other men. He tried to count the number involved, but they moved too quick-ly.

He needed a distraction. Something to make them pause just long enough for the other men to grab hold of them. He wasn't about to fire a revolver inside the hotel, although the clatter from that would certainly have stopped the fight. He'd have to settle for something much simpler.

"Hey!" he shouted in a booming voice. It tore through the room, and every man paused. It was just long enough for the hotel employees to pin a few of the men. Two of the others recovered more quickly and began throwing punches again. He strode toward them, and before either could react to his presence, he hit one square in the jaw and the other in the stomach.

"This hotel is no place for a brawl." He ground the words through his teeth as pain shot through his knuckles. "Hold on to them." He directed the last words to the two employees who'd been trying to pull the men apart.

Clenching and unclenching his right hand, he moved around the mess to McFarland, who was still kneeling on the floor, holding his prisoner. "Have you got a place where these men can cool off?" he asked McFarland.

"We've a few spare rooms. Or I suppose we could put them in the outbuild-ings." McFarland's words came in puffs of breath as he worked to keep the other man down.

"Either will do." James pulled a revolver and held it at the man on the floor to allow McFarland to stand. The scruffy-looking fellow remained in place. A quick appraisal of each of the men involved in the brawl showed none of them to be armed. "All of you," he said, turning to address the men being held. "Fol-low McFarland. You step out of line, I won't hesitate to make you regret it."

One by one, the men stood, the employees backing off slowly. A few of the brawlers looked the worse for their poor decisions. As he waited, the crowd murmured around him, reminding him he had an audience. James quickly scanned the onlookers to ensure there would be no more trouble.

His eyes immediately landed on one of the waitresses standing near the front of the crowd. While her friends chattered, she observed the scene silently, her gaze finally finding James. She gave him a timid smile, and that one little look somehow brightened his entire mood. He stood straighter, and his voice boomed even louder when he told the men to hurry along.

Even as he followed the group down the north wing hallway, he felt her gaze on his back. And when he returned from seeing the men locked into vari-ous rooms and outbuildings, she was still standing in the lobby, even as an old-er woman shooed the waitresses back into the dining room. He paused in the middle of the floor, half wanting to speak with her—about what, though, he hadn't the faintest idea—and half wanting to turn and run.

He didn't have to make a decision, however, because she found her way to-ward him, gliding across the floor as if at a fancy ball somewhere back East. When she stood in front of him, she pushed her spectacles up the bridge of her nose just slightly. It was an adorable gesture, a tiny thing she likely wasn't even aware she did, and James fought to keep from smiling like a lunatic.

"That was very brave of you," she finally said, her voice soft as a breeze across the prairie grasses back home.

"It's what I'm here for. But thank you," he said. He glanced behind him to-ward the hallway where some of the men had been taken. "Do you know what they were fighting over?"

She shook her head. "I was serving dinner. We all heard a racket and came to see what was happening out here. I'd seen you leave earlier, and so Genia and

I ran to find you." She grinned and chewed her lip. "I'll likely hear about how dangerous it was to run outside in the twilight hours from Mrs. Ruby later."

The stern-faced woman who had bustled most of the other girls back into the dining room still stood near the doors, her eagle eyes sweeping the lobby and gesturing at waitresses as she saw them. "Would that be the terrifying Mrs. Ruby?" James asked, nodding at the woman.

Miss Dutton turned, and then quickly looked back at him, sheepish. "It is. And I should go before I find myself in even more trouble." She reached for his hand and squeezed it. "Thank you again, Deputy Wright. We are all grateful you're here." Then she dropped his hand and made her way quickly toward Mrs. Ruby.

He stood absolutely dumbfounded in the middle of the room. She'd taken his hand. He held it up for a moment. It looked no different, yet it felt . . . empty.

He shook his head and dropped his hand to his side. He must look quite the fool standing here in the lobby, staring at his hand as if it were a foreign thing.

"Deputy Wright?" McFarland called his name from near the front desk. "Some of those fellows seem to have cooled off enough if you wish to speak with them." The man's light Irish brogue spurred James into motion.

He was here to work, not to moon after pretty, brown-eyed girls who took his hand for approximately three seconds. And with his mind finally straight—or as straight as it could get—he set off to find out the reason for the brawl in the hotel.

Chapter Eight

The lunch service the next day was so busy, Edie barely had time to think in between tables. As soon as she took one table's order, she had to pour water and coffee for the next and bring out food for another and remove the setting for yet another. Despite how quickly she had to move, she actually preferred services like this one. They went by quickly, and they didn't leave much time for conversation. As adept as Edie was at crafting clever conversation, even with the roughest of men, she much preferred not to since it inevitably found her needing to lie about her past.

The service had just begun slowing down long after the southbound train left the depot. Edie finished pouring hot coffee for a gentleman at a corner table and turned to greet a new guest at a table by one of the large windows.

"Deputy Wright," she exclaimed. "I haven't seen you eat in the dining room before." She wanted to grip the edge of the table for support, since she suddenly felt as if she weren't quite herself. But that wouldn't do, and so she placed both hands on the handle of the coffeepot.

"I'm usually in more of a hurry, but today I thought I might take it easier."

"Did the tea I left not work for your headaches?" She'd read about the use of sagebrush leaves among the Indians to ease head pains. And she'd found the peppermint she'd read about in the kitchen pantry. Chef had been none too thrilled to allow her to search through his goods, but when she told him who they were for, he relented. It seemed everyone was grateful for Deputy Wright's presence in Crest Stone. And after what had happened yesterday, Edie was too. At least she was when she didn't think too much about how interested he might be in her family.

Her family. They couldn't be the ones who'd come into the Territory. Her father had once said he'd never leave Kansas. Unless he had a reason to leave . . . A ripple of panic raced through her. It wasn't the first time she'd had that thought since Deputy Wright had told her about what he'd heard. The fear had been ever-present in the back of her mind since then, causing her to be even more mindful of her surroundings.

"I have yet to try them as I haven't experienced one since yesterday morning I only meant that I thought I might take my time over lunch rather than rushing about." He paused, picked up the cutlery in front of him as if he would use it, and then put it back down. "I want to thank you for the herbs. It was very kind."

"Oh, you're welcome." Edie's cheeks went warm. She stood there, thoughts of her family forced away, and feeling as if she'd forgotten every bit of waitressing training she'd received. She looked down at her hands, and her brain chugged along like the train leaving the depot. She finally realized she should offer the man something to drink. "Would you care for some coffee?"

He nodded and slid the cup and saucer across the table. Her fingers grazed his as she gripped the mug. It brought to mind the impulsive way she'd grabbed his hand yesterday. She bit down hard on her lip as she poured, hoping to dispel the memory—and the blush that was surely creeping back up into her cheeks. The man was going to begin to think she had a medical condition if she kept flushing at every word and thought.

"Were you in much trouble for coming to get me yesterday?" he asked, taking the cup in his hands.

"No, thankfully." Although Beatrice had warned her that Mrs. Ruby had spotted her speaking with the deputy after the commotion in the lobby, Mrs. Ruby hadn't said anything. Edie hoped that meant she only thought Edie was thanking the man for coming. And indeed, Mrs. Ruby had been grateful to Edie and Genia for acting quickly. But Edie knew she needed to be more careful in the future—and now. She glanced about the room, even though she remembered Mrs. Ruby had gone to her office not too long ago. "We were all very impressed with how you stepped into the middle of the melee. The girls and I, that is."

Deputy Wright sipped his coffee. "It's what I'm supposed to do."

Edie paused, curiosity catching her thoughts. She should tell the man the lunch offerings and check on her other tables. But with the family she'd had, where lawmen were considered something akin to the Devil himself, she was truly curious about what motivated one to follow the path Deputy Wright had. "May I ask you a question?"

He set his coffee down and gave her a slight smile. "Certainly."

"What made you want to work for the county sheriff?" The moment it was out of her mouth, it felt much too intrusive. She searched for something to mitigate the bluntness of her question. "Considering how dangerous it is, I mean."

He sat back and arranged the napkin in his lap. "It is dangerous, I suppose, although I don't often think of it that way." He looked her up and down, as if assessing whether she was worthy of knowing more about his motivations.

Edie held still, waiting for his response.

"My uncle Mark was a county sheriff back in Kansas. He was dedicated to his work, and very good at it too. My family were farmers; they never quite understood why my uncle would put himself in harm's way the way he did." He glanced down at the napkin again, as if thinking. "He was a good man—a great man. He often came around for supper, and we'd talk for hours. He understood me in a way no one else in my family did. So I suppose he's the reason I came here, looking for work with whoever might take me on."

Edie swallowed. It was a moving story, and she identified with how he felt about his parents. "He sounds wonderful."

"He was."

The past tense didn't escape Edie's notice. "I'm so sorry."

Deputy Wright looked up at her, the ghost of a smile there to reassure her. "Don't be. I was happy to have known him while I could."

Beyond the table, the sun streamed in through the window as it did every day, not caring who was here to see it and who wasn't. Edie wished with all her heart she had someone like Deputy Wright's uncle, even if it meant she'd suffer a loss as deeply as he did. "I have no one like that," she said softly.

"I'm sorry," he said. "Everyone deserves at least one person who understands them."

She drew her gaze from the window back to him. He was watching her with curious eyes. She'd already said too much, lingered too long, and become far more involved than she'd ever intended. "I must attend to my other tables." She whipped around, but before she could take a step, he spoke.

"May I at least place an order for my lunch?" His voice was teasing, but Edie closed her eyes in embarrassment. Some Gilbert Girl she was, taking plenty of time to inquire about personal matters that were none of her concern while neglecting her responsibilities.

She nodded mutely as he asked for beef and barley soup and bread, forcing herself to repeat the order in her head over and over because she felt certain she'd forget it otherwise. Then she bustled back to the kitchen to place the order and catch her breath. What had possessed her to demand so much from him?

It felt as if she'd crossed some dangerous line, and now she wasn't certain she could return to the other side.

Chapter Nine

Early the next morning, James woke with a dull ache pressing against his brow. This was the third in only a few days. A flash of impatience raced through him, until he remembered the herbs Miss Dutton had left him. And so he dressed and found his way to the lunch counter where he retrieved a cup of hot water. While he waited for the herbs to steep, he tried to focus on penning a telegram to Sheriff Young, letting him know of the fight and asking for any news about the men from Kansas.

With the telegram written out, James held the steaming liquid under his nose. The peppermint scent overpowered any other potential odor the tea might have had. He took a tentative sip. It was bitter but not undrinkable, which was how he thought of most tea. He drank the remainder of it and gathered his things.

If Miss Dutton's concoction worked, he'd owe her more than he could ever pay. His condition had cost him many a day's work over the years, and if people knew of it, he'd never be elected to any office, much less that of a town marshal. Folks generally preferred their lawmen to be ready to act at any moment, not lying in bed, afflicted with debilitating headaches.

James returned the cup to the lunch counter—and accepted a small pastry from Miss Barnett—on his way out the door. He paused a moment in the lobby to put on his coat. There was no sign of Miss Dutton, and he found himself disappointed not to tell her he'd tried her herbs. He wondered how long it would be before they began to take effect. The pain was still dull, and it came and went, which meant he had at least a small window of time in which to send his telegram and—if he were lucky—venture down into the town.

Outside, the vibrant green of the spring grasses waved in a chill breeze. The sounds of hammers and an occasional shout echoed up from around the railroad tracks, indicating men had already gone to work on the new buildings.

James strode down the path worn by daily carriage wheels from the hotel to the depot.

Behind the office window in the small depot, young Christopher Rennet stood ready to assist customers. Behind him, James spotted the depot clerk, Mr. Thomason, working at the telegraph machine. James unfolded the note he'd written Sheriff Young, and passed it to Christopher, along with payment.

"Is it urgent?" Christopher asked after glancing at the recipient of James's note. "Mr. Thomason's got a bunch of messages to send."

James shook his head. "Not particularly. How about you bring me any response up to the hotel later on?"

"I will, sir. As fast as I can."

James forced himself not to laugh at the boy's sincerity. Instead, he gave him a serious nod and an extra coin. The boy's eyes grew round, and James knew he'd have his reply as fast as Christopher's legs could carry him.

As he stepped outside, he assessed his situation again. The pain remained slight, noticeable but not unmanageable. It hadn't worsened. Miss Dutton's herbs must be working.

James marveled at her knowledge. But it was more than that, considering she'd also had to gather the right plants in the correct amounts and pound them into the right size. It was a skill she had, and one that might allow him to do his job instead of hiding in his room all day.

James took his time strolling through the burgeoning town. He greeted the men he'd met already, and learned the names of a few new faces. In addition to the land office and the bank, a livery stable was going up on the other side of the smithy's shack, and a boarding house—the owner of which proudly proclaimed to James that his rooms would be much cheaper than the hotel's—and a small home (for the banker, one of the men building the place informed James) were also under construction. And seemingly overnight, the skeleton of yet another building had begun to take shape.

He was determined to meet the Hartley he'd heard of, and one of the men working on the banker's home pointed him behind the mercantile. James walked in that direction, past the muddy area where Miss Dutton had taken a tumble. The memory brought a smile to his face, although he doubted it would to hers. Behind the barn that sat to the rear of the mercantile, he found two men standing in a seemingly empty space of grass and sage.

"Good morning," he called. "I hear one of you is Monroe Hartley?"

The taller of the two men stepped forward and held out a hand. "I'm Hartley. And this is my foreman, Jim Daley." He nodded toward the rounder man to his right.

James shook both their hands. "James Wright, county sheriff's deputy."

"You broke up that fight at the hotel yesterday," Hartley said with an approving nod. "We're glad to have you here. Will you be staying?"

"Only until the town can elect its own marshal," James replied. "I've been told you're the one in charge of most of this building."

"You'd be correct. I did the hotel, and I've been hired on to do the land office, the bank, and the banker's house. I've got a few more folks interested in hiring me on."

"Word about this place is spreading," Daley added.

"I'd say." James surveyed the land on which they stood. "You planning on putting something here?"

Hartley smiled. "Just a home for myself and my wife. She's expecting our first child."

"Congratulations. This is a good spot."

Hartley's eyes scanned the land around him with pride. "I thought so. And she approved of it. I already bought it from the railroad. All I have to do now is build it before the baby arrives."

"You need any help, just say the word."

"You might have just got yourself another job," the foreman joked.

"I appreciate that, Deputy," Hartley said. "I'll let you know if we do."

They talked a little longer about building and about the town. And when James left, he realized the headache was still nothing but a ghost of its usual cruel self. A smile crossed his face as he reached the mercantile. Miss Dutton was a miracle worker, and he couldn't wait to tell her.

Chapter Ten

The sun hadn't yet risen when Edie stood, huddled in her coat, near the hotel stables with the other Gilbert Company employees who had the day off and wished to attend Sunday services in Cañon City. Even though it was much earlier than most of the waitresses were used to rising, there was an air of anticipation among the group as many of them hadn't been since before the snow began falling last autumn. The hotel couldn't afford to let all its staff take each Sunday off, so among the Gilbert Girls, those with the most seniority received more Sundays off than the newer waitresses. Somewhere in the middle, Edie had two Sundays free each month.

McFarland, the stable hands, and several of the men worked to secure the horses to all four of the hotel's wagons. Normally, they'd be used to transport goods from the depot or the mercantile, but today, they were to provide transportation for the ride to Cañon City. Boards had been laid across the wagon boxes to provide seating. Edie flexed her frozen fingers inside her gloves. As cold as it was, she was looking forward to the ride. She was likely the only woman waiting who didn't wish the Colorado & New Mexico Railway Company would add another run—only on Sunday mornings—to allow them to travel more quickly.

When the horses were hitched, the girls around Edie began climbing into the nearest wagon. The last to join them, she found herself sitting in the front. It wasn't such a bad seat. While it would be difficult to converse with the other girls on the long ride, she'd have a wonderful view of the scenery once the sun rose.

The driver swung himself onto the bench next to her, and before she had a moment to find out who it was, he called across to McFarland in a smooth, deep voice.

Edie's face instantly went red in pre-dawn dark. Deputy Wright. What was he doing here? He didn't work for the hotel. She couldn't decide if she was annoyed or pleasantly surprised. She tucked her hands together and hoped he couldn't sense anything she felt. He nudged the horses into motion, and their wagon fell in line behind the other two.

"Good morning," he finally said.

"Good morning, Deputy," she replied, happy that at least her voice sounded perfectly normal, even if her hands were jittery and her mind wouldn't settle.

"Miss Dutton." His smile was evident in his voice, and that, in turn, made Edie smile too. "It's a pleasure to see you again."

Edie couldn't feel the chill of the morning anymore, not with those words. She told herself it was nothing but pleasantries, and that he might have said it sitting next to anyone, but that didn't stop the wave of warm happiness that flooded her body. It was dangerous, being thankful for more time to speak with this man, but that old fear seemed so far away at the moment. "Thank you. How have you been?"

"I'm in excellent health, all because of your herbs."

"They worked?" she exclaimed before she realized it might sound to him as if she hadn't the slightest idea what she was doing. And, well, that might be right to a degree. She'd experimented some at home, but so many plants here were new to her.

"They did, thank you." He tilted his head as he looked at her. "Should I be concerned?"

"Not at all," she said, more confidently than she felt. "I spent many a day working with plants at home." Different plants, of course, but he didn't need to know that. After all, she'd consulted Mrs. McFarland's books to ensure she'd chosen the correct herbs.

"I believe you may have a talent for healing," he said.

Edie scoffed. "I'm happy as a Gilbert Girl. It's more than I could have ever hoped for."

They were quiet for a few moments while the wagon rolled through the darkness. Behind them, the girls chattered quietly, but as Edie peered out across the valley, the same old uneasiness came creeping back into her mind. "Deputy Wright, have you heard anything else about the men from Kansas?" she asked quietly, so as not to alarm any of the girls.

"I haven't," he replied. "I'll check with the sheriff before we leave town to-day, but his last telegram indicated nothing new."

Edie relaxed some. Perhaps it was nothing but an accidental foray into the Territory and they'd already returned to Kansas. She'd say extra prayers at services today, just in case.

It was funny how quickly such a thing as churchgoing could grow on a person. Before coming to the hotel, Edie had never set foot inside a church. She'd never had the opportunity. But when all the other girls seemed eager to go, Edie went too, mostly so as not to draw attention to herself for *not* attending. It was uncomfortable at first, not knowing the hymns and not understanding how it all worked. But after a few Sundays, she'd settled into the routine and found herself looking forward to the peaceful moments and the sermon. Somehow, the preacher always seemed to be speaking to her, even though he had no idea who she was.

"Miss Dutton?"

Edie started. "Yes, I'm sorry. I was lost in thought."

Deputy Wright smiled at her. "I was only telling you that I heard yesterday that a minister might be on his way to Crest Stone. If that's the truth, it won't be long before a church is built and you'll no longer need to travel to Cañon City on Sundays."

"Oh."

"You don't sound particularly excited. One might think you actually enjoy this jostling, hours-long drive." His voice was teasing, and it made Edie smile.

"Would you think me crazy if I said I do?"

"Not at all. Different, yes, but not crazy. It is a beautiful ride, and, I imagine, a change from your daily work."

It was as if he could read her mind. That ought to make her worry, but instead it put Edie at ease. "I suppose you also enjoy this ride?"

"Is it terrible that I wished the railroad hadn't come through here so I could've ridden down?"

"Quite terrible," she said with a grin.

"I suppose I shouldn't wish for such a thing. After all, it makes it easier for folks to do business, travel, and to visit friends and family."

"Does your family come to visit you?" she asked.

Deputy Wright was quiet a moment, and Edie almost wished she hadn't asked. He'd mentioned his family didn't understand his choosing to become a lawman. Maybe he'd left them on unhappy terms.

"No," he finally said. "They don't much leave the farm and the little town nearby. Besides, they didn't approve of my career choice." He gave her a half-grin that she suspected was forced.

"I understand," she said.

Deputy Wright raised his eyebrows. He looked as if he wanted to ask her why, but she turned away. Toward the east, the first light of dawn was just beginning to show over the tops of the smooth Wet Mountains. It wouldn't be long before it filled the valley with soft rays.

"Bonnieville," he said, out of nowhere.

"I'm sorry?" Edie turned back toward him.

"The town near my parents' farm. It's where I grew up. Are you familiar with it?"

Edie searched her memory but came up empty. "I'm not. Where is it?"

"Northeast of Topeka. How about you? Whereabouts did you grow up?" He asked the question as he shifted the lines in his hands.

Edie chewed on her lip, trying to decide how much truth to tell him. She settled on a story that was as close as she could get. "All around. We lived in several different areas." Feeling as if she needed to explain why, she added, "My parents liked to try their luck with new ventures."

"That must have been hard." His voice was so full of empathy, Edie felt bad for not being entirely truthful. Which was a ridiculous thought. If she told him the honest truth, he'd likely never speak to her again—or worse, suspect she was just like her father, her uncle, and her brothers.

"It was," she said carefully as she unnecessarily retied the ribbons from her hat that looped under her chin. When she snuck a glance at him, he was watching her with nothing but compassion written across his face. No one had ever looked at her that way. Pity, yes, but rarely compassion. When she'd gotten caught in Mr. Adkins's plot, she'd seen a lot of pity. Which was better than anger, but if she could live the rest of her life without anyone pitying her ever again, she'd be happy. Dora had been compassionate toward her, but it was something different than what she saw now with Deputy Wright.

"How long has it been since you lost them?" he asked.

Edie wrapped her hands together. She'd almost forgotten she'd said such a thing to him. Except . . . She hadn't really. She'd told him she had no family left in Kansas, which he understood to mean they'd died. She could let him continue to think that, but the thought of such a blatant lie made her insides feel as if they'd just ridden the wagon over a large rock. She glanced at him again and decided to go with as much truth as possible. "My family is alive. I'm sorry if I made you think otherwise. I meant only that I . . . that they no longer wish to speak to me. I suppose they didn't approve of my choice either." She kept her eyes on her hands, afraid that if she looked up, she might give away more of the story.

Deputy Wright didn't speak. Instead, he reached a gloved hand over, covered her clasped hands with his and squeezed. It was the most natural, comforting thing he could have done, and it took a few seconds for Edie to realize that it *shouldn't* be done. He seemed to come to the same conclusion and drew his hand away quickly, leaving her feeling strangely alone.

She forced herself to breathe as she listened to the girls talk behind her. No one said anything, and at no point did their conversation pause to indicate they'd seen the deputy reach for her hand. She let out a shuddering breath.

Deputy Wright cleared his throat. "I was the only boy my parents had. My father wanted me to take over his farm, but I never much cared for it. I was always more interested in my uncle Mark's stories of chasing down outlaws and breaking up saloon fights. After he died . . . Well, I was lost for a while. But then I made up my mind to follow in his footsteps and set out for the Colorado Territory in the hopes of finding work as a deputy somewhere. I don't think my father has ever forgiven me."

"But surely he's proud of you, even if he doesn't say it," Edie replied. "All fathers are proud of their sons." Her own father certainly was, even when they acted up. Of course, they'd all followed the path he'd laid out for them, and joined up with him as soon as they were able to shoot straight and ride for hours on end. And as soon as Mama would let them go, of course, which seemed to be later and later with each boy.

Deputy Wright didn't say anything right away. Instead, he sat straight up on the bench, his jaw set and his eyes on the horses. In the soft glow of dawn, she could see the faint shadow of the beginnings of a beard. She couldn't imagine anyone thinking less of this man. He was brave, kind, and terribly good looking. He could easily reach over and pull her closer to him on the bench without even slowing the horses. A rush of heat flooded Edie from her face to her toes as she imagined such a thing.

She was getting carried away with herself. She needed to force herself to treat him just as she treated every other man who came into the hotel restaurant. That was safe. That was reasonable.

But she was beginning to think she'd somehow already strayed far from the safe and reasonable path. And, when she glanced up at him, she wasn't certain she could find her way back—or if she even wanted to.

Chapter Eleven

They reached Cañon City just before eleven o'clock. As they'd grown closer, James dreaded the end of the ride. And this time, it had nothing to do with the scenery or rocking of the wagon. Instead, it had everything to do with the petite woman sitting next to him.

He could barely look at her as the sun had risen in the sky. The way it illuminated the ivory of her skin and the bright strands of her hair made him want to stop the buckboard, grab her hand, and go running off to the mountains with her.

By the time they'd reached town, he thought he might be losing his mind.

James climbed down from the wagon at the livery stables and walked to the side to help the other ladies down. A couple of them blushed when they took his hand, but James only smiled and wished them a good day before rushing back around to Miss Dutton. He held out a hand for her, which she clasped. He marveled at how small her hand was compared to his. Something about it made him feel fiercely protective.

As she went to step down from the wagon, the toe of her shoe caught the edge of the wood. She stumbled forward, straight into him. Instinctively, he wrapped his arms around her waist, holding her to him. He set her down gently—ignoring the voice in the back of his head that wanted to hold on to her just a moment longer. "Are you all right?" he asked.

"Y-yes," she stammered. She busied herself with arranging her skirts and shifting the reticule that looped around her wrist. She didn't look at him, but he thought he caught a slight smile as her head ducked to examine the hem of her coat. "Thank you," she added, still not looking at him.

"Shall I escort you to the church?" he asked.

Her head jerked up and her eyes flickered to the others in their group—the McFarlands, other waitresses, some maids, and a few male employees of the hotel—before returning to land on him again. "Thank you, Deputy Wright, but I'm not certain that would be proper." She gave him the sweetest smile even as she turned him down.

"I understand." He did, a little, but what he really wanted to do was take Miss Dutton's arm in his and tell McFarland to stuff his rules.

She moved in front of him, skirts swaying under her coat as she joined a couple of her friends. James trailed behind, his emotions running in what felt like six different directions as they walked down the plank sidewalk and into the church. He sat at the end of one pew, Miss Dutton a few seats down in front of him. She knelt and bowed her head, reminding him he should do the same.

But he didn't know what to pray for, beyond guidance in his work. Praying for Miss Dutton felt self-serving, even more than if he prayed for himself. So instead, he quickly sat back down and tried to parse through his thoughts before the service began.

But even that seemed beyond his abilities right now. He felt restless and agitated. His eyes kept wandering to Miss Dutton, even after the service began. She was beautiful, but more than that, she possessed humility, and that made her even more attractive. Each moment he spent with her brought her even further into the forefront of his thoughts. How could he work if he was thinking of her all the time? It was dangerous. Uncle Mark had fallen head over heels for a woman who had brought him to his death.

Edie isn't like that. The thought echoed over and over. And it was true. Edie was no snake, sent to lure him into a trap the way Uncle Mark had been. But wouldn't the end result be the same? If he was so distracted by thoughts of her, he wouldn't be able to focus on everything else around him. And he had to remain vigilant if he was to keep peace in Crest Stone and prove himself worthy of being town marshal.

But at the same time, how could he ignore the obvious connection he felt with Miss Dutton? He hadn't expected them to have such similar backgrounds. When she told him about her family, he knew immediately that she understood how he felt. It was a terrible thing, to carry around the disappointment of the people who raised and loved you before anyone else did. At times, he felt as if he were some sort of traitor, or as if he'd done his father an irreparable wrong by leaving to pursue his own ideals. Even though she hadn't said it out loud, he could sense Edie felt the same.

He couldn't believe he'd reached for her hand in the buckboard. He hadn't even thought about what he was doing; it was as if the action were out of his control. If anyone had seen it, she could have lost her position. It was a foolish action. He needed to ensure it didn't happen again—even if he wanted it to.

The sermon seemed to drag, and when it finally ended, James hadn't the slightest notion about what the preacher had said. While others in the congregation waited to speak with the preacher and shake his hand, James pulled his hat on and slid out the door as quickly as possible. He needed to move, to do something, and to stop thinking.

He strode in the direction of the sheriff's office. The exercise, chill air, and the scent of horse dung cleared his head some, as did nodding and greeting passersby who recognized him. He had a couple of hours before he needed to return to the livery stables; McFarland told him the hotel employees always enjoyed taking time to shop and have lunch in town before returning home. He'd speak with Ben about the men from Kansas, give him an update on what was happening in Crest Stone, and find out about anything new happening in Cañon City.

James wiped the mud and dung off his boots before turning the doorknob to enter the sheriff's office. He found Ben locking up a sputtering, scarred man in one of the cells in the rear of the building.

"What'd that one do?" he asked, keeping a wary distance from the man after seeing him spit once through the bars of the cell.

"Tried to make off with a horse tied up out front of Murray's," Ben said, pocketing the key to the cell.

"Weren't no one using it!" the man yelled from behind the bars of his cell.

Ben ignored him and shut the door that separated the cells from the office. "Didn't expect you back up here so soon," he said to James.

"McFarland needed another man to drive one of the wagons to Sunday services." An image of Edie sitting next to him, the orange glow of the sun making her look like some kind of angel, came to mind. James had to shake his head to make it disappear. "Thought it might be a good opportunity to check in with you. Anything new happening around here?"

"It's been more quiet than usual," Ben said, tossing the cell keys onto the desk and taking a seat behind it. "I can't help but think it's the quiet before the storm."

James sat in the chair opposite. "That sounds dire. You expecting trouble?"

"Not expecting it, but there's something in the air. I can't place it." Ben leaned forward in his chair and sorted through a small stack of papers.

James sat forward too, elbows on his knees. "Anything to do with those men from Kansas?"

"Might be." Ben pulled a few wanted posters from the stack of papers and handed them to James. "There've been rumblings of trouble east of here. Still a ways off, but enough to make me take notice. I heard yesterday about a stage robbery southeast of Pueblo. And this morning, Old Jack over at the telegraph office told me the Huerfano County sheriff's been up to his ears in reports of stolen horses and brawls in out of the way places, moving westward across the county."

James scanned through the posters, recognizing old names and faces. Levi Fletcher. Tell Fletcher. Jonas Beaumont. Ty Beaumont. Nick Ford, related in some way to the Beaumonts through marriage. The faces and the names lit up a caged fire deep down inside. What were they doing in Colorado?

"You ever run into them in Kansas?" Ben asked.

"Not directly." James pressed his lips together as the old anger—the one he'd thought he'd dealt with when he became a deputy here—coursed through him again. He rolled up the posters and forced the feeling down. "Does anyone know which family it is?"

"Can't say as I've heard," Ben replied. "Is one worse than the other?"

James grimaced. "Not particularly. The Fletchers are more prone to violence, but the Beaumonts are more devious. Neither one of them is easy to catch." He should know. He'd spent far longer in Kansas than he meant to after Uncle Mark's death, trying to do exactly that. It got him nothing but dust and frustration.

"I wonder what they're after." Ben tapped his fingers on the stack of papers.

"Could be anything. Could be that it's gotten too hot in Kansas for them and they're here to bide their time."

"I'll keep my ear to the ground and wire you if I hear anything new. How's it going in Crest Stone?"

"Good," James said as the front door to the building opened. "Been busy." He turned to see who'd come in as Ben rose from his seat.

"You didn't miss much," Mrs. Young said, waltzing in to give her husband a kiss on the cheek. A trail of ladies—all waitresses from the hotel in Crest Stone—followed behind her. James stood to greet them. The last woman in shut the door behind her, and James froze in place.

There was no mistaking the soft yellow dress and the sheer joy that seemed to radiate from her face. She was quieter than the other girls, but more striking than any of them. Miss Dutton spotted James and gave him a smile. He stood rooted to his place and only just barely heard Mrs. Young speaking to him.

"I heard you were quite the gallant gentleman, offering to drive the girls up from the hotel to church," she said. "We're going to have a visit. You're both welcome to join us."

"I'm afraid I've some correspondence to catch up on, and then I have rounds to make," Ben said.

"James?" Mrs. Young turned to him. "Would you care to join us?"

He had to tear his eyes away from Miss Dutton—only to find Mrs. Young glancing back and forth between him and Miss Dutton, and Ben giving him a curious look.

One of the girls giggled and whispered into the ear of another one beside her, and James had the urge to run.

"I can't. I'm sorry. Got to help . . . I have to go." He scooped up his hat and coat and pushed past the group, purposefully not looking at Miss Dutton as he passed her, even though it seemed as if he could feel her presence separate from that of anyone else.

The door shut behind him and he strode down the plank sidewalk, not even pausing as he shrugged on his coat.

His distraction was becoming a preoccupation.

Chapter Twelve

" Edie, wake up. You're going to miss breakfast."

Edie opened her eyes to see Beatrice standing over her, already dressed. She sat up, feeling as if she'd slept for days. "I'm sorry. I must have been exhausted from yesterday."

Beatrice glanced at the small clock that sat on the vanity table. "If you hurry, I'll wait for you."

Edie leapt out of bed and went through the motions of preparing for the day as visions of all that had happened yesterday filled her head. The ride to Cañon City, where she'd discovered she and Deputy Wright had more in common than she ever could have thought. The church service, where she struggled to pay attention to the sermon because he sat behind her. Running into him again at the sheriff's office. The way the other girls teased her about him after that uncomfortable moment where it seemed he couldn't take his eyes off her. How Penny had pulled her aside afterward and insisted upon every detail, which Edie had given only sparingly. The ride home, in which she sat in a different wagon but seemed acutely aware of Deputy Wright's every movement in the wagon behind them. And then being unable to fall asleep until late last night because of these exact thoughts.

Despite the chaos in her mind, Edie was ready to leave for breakfast in record time. When they reached the landing at the top of the stairs, she paused, looking out over the people who had begun appearing in the lobby. It was early, so there weren't many yet.

"Searching for someone?" Beatrice asked with a teasing smile.

"No." But it was a lie, of course. She desperately needed something else to occupy her mind. Something that didn't have piercing green eyes or a smile that seemed only for her.

"It's nothing to be ashamed of," Beatrice said. "If it makes you feel any better, there's a gentleman who always seems to sit at one of my tables, not at all by accident. And I don't mind one bit."

"I didn't know you were such a flirt!" Edie teased.

Beatrice laughed. "I'm not! All I'm saying is that it's not so terrible if you have a man who takes an interest in you. So long as Mrs. Ruby doesn't find out."

"That's what I'd fear," Edie said. That, and Deputy Wright learning her true name. She wasn't certain which would be worse.

"Well, I think you should enjoy it. Don't get carried away like Millie, but there's no harm in it otherwise."

"Poor Millie. I don't think this new gentleman she has her sights on is going to turn out much better than any of the other men she keeps falling for," Edie said. Millie was quite adept at getting her heart broken. How she'd had a string of beaux without losing her position was something Edie couldn't figure out.

Beatrice led the way downstairs, and together the girls walked toward the kitchen—until they came upon posters nailed to the wall beside the front desk. Posters Edie normally would've given only a cursory glance as a reassurance, but that today, made her freeze.

"Are you all right?" Beatrice had stopped a few feet ahead.

"I . . ." She tore her eyes from the wall and forced herself to look at Beatrice. "I'm fine. I only forgot my . . . hat." Indeed she had forgotten her hat in her rush to leave for breakfast, even if that wasn't the reason she stopped.

"Well, I'm famished. I'll see you in the kitchen." Beatrice disappeared quickly around the corner into the hallway that led to the kitchen door.

Edie stood a moment, searching the few people in the lobby to ensure she saw no familiar faces. And then she turned slowly back to the posters. She pushed her glasses into place and scanned all five of them. Two of the Fletchers were pinned up top, but below that, sketches of faces she'd known her entire life stared back at her. Jonas Beaumont. Ty Beaumont. Nick Ford.

Pa. Ty, her oldest brother. Cousin Nick.

Edie's stomach rolled and she gripped the edge of the front desk to keep from toppling over. It was them. Her family. The ones she thought had no idea where she was.

But clearly they did. And they were coming for her.

Her heart racing, Edie moved toward the stairs as fast as she could without drawing attention to herself, only to stop short again when she overheard a snippet of a conversation happening at the front desk. She paused at the bottom of the stairs, pretending to retie her apron as she willed her heart to stop pounding so hard.

"What did they get?" the desk clerk was asking the rough-looking man standing at the counter.

"Bunch of nothing, so far as I heard. Broke a window at the company office, though. The foreman is steaming mad." The man leaned against the desk, his dirty coat swaying around him.

"Those miners don't know a good thing when they've got it."

The man shrugged. "Heard it was some newcomer that got them all riled up. Started a brawl in the saloon, then went off and tried to get rich."

Edie grabbed hold of the banister and dug her fingers into the wood. Her mind sped in circles. Nothing made Nick happier than a brawl, though the rest of her kin preferred to stay on the edges of things like that. But the Fletchers . . . They were on that wall too. And everyone knew how given they were toward a fight. It could be them. Or it could just be miners.

Or it could be Nick. And if was Nick, her father and brothers were nearby.

Edie pulled herself up the stairs. She could stay put. Stay here and hope for the best. After all, no one here knew Edith Beaumont. They knew Edie Dutton. But if Mr. Adkins had called her bluff and given her location away to her family . . . They would be coming for her.

And unless she wanted to return to Kansas, she'd need to run.

Chapter Thirteen

It was just about the edge of dusk when James let the horse he'd borrowed from the hotel into the corral at the mining camp's makeshift livery. He didn't much trust leaving the saddle and other tack behind in this place, but he couldn't very well carry it about the camp. He settled for stowing it in a dark corner of the livery, under some moldering blankets.

The horse taken care of, he strolled out into the camp. The place consisted of a few patched-together buildings, sheets of dirty canvas held up with poles that acted as shelters, and a lot of churned-up mud. It didn't take long to spot the mine company office and its attached marshal's office. They were the nicest buildings in the camp, although that was still saying a lot about them.

After speaking with the camp's marshal, a short, burly man who'd once been a Texas ranger but found private work to be more lucrative, James emerged onto the main thoroughfare with an air of relief. The trouble he'd heard of happening last night had been nothing but a bunch of drunken miners fighting in the saloon and then attempting to break into the company store. When they couldn't get in there, they broke one of the rear windows in the office. Sheriff Tate then promptly arrested all seven of them and stowed them in his jail. James took a moment to speak with them, but it quickly became clear not a one of them was connected in any way to the Kansas gangs.

This knowledge made it possible that the rumors of the Fletchers or the Beaumonts coming into Colorado were still only just rumors. If he were honest with himself, nothing would make him happier than to put every last Fletcher into prison—or a noose—for what they'd done to his uncle, but he'd put the thirst for vengeance behind him a long time ago. He'd spent a year of his life searching for those men. An entire wasted year, until he realized his uncle would have hated that. When he left Kansas, he not only left his parents and sisters behind, but also the desire to see the Fletchers brought to justice.

He refused to let those old feelings derail him here.

Night in the camp brought out men eager to part with their meager earnings, and James dodged miners in all states of drink and mood on his way back to the livery. He wasn't but twenty feet away from the corral when he spotted a large man hulking over a boy, his finger in the kid's face, and yelling at the top of his lungs.

"I know you took it. I ain't had it set down for but a minute, and you're the only one who was in there." The man's voice carried the telltale slur of one too many swigs of whiskey.

The boy backed up against the rough wooden wall of the stables, his eyes searching left and right for a way out.

"You ain't gonna give it back to me, I'll find it myself." The bigger man reached for the boy's pocket, pressing his other hand against the kid's throat when he tried to squirrel away. The boy let out a startled gasp and clutched the man's arm with his hands, seemingly trying to push him back. But the bigger man held tight and thrust his hand into the boy's pocket, looking for whatever item he'd lost.

The boy began banging frantically on the man's arm, and that was when James had seen enough. It was one thing to search the kid's pocket, but another entirely to put his life in danger.

"Hey!" he shouted as he strode toward them.

His voice startled the man enough that he slackened his grip on the boy, although not enough for the kid to make an escape. "What do you want?" the man almost growled at him.

"Just making sure you aren't hurting this boy." James took another step closer as the man's eyes landed on the badge pinned to James's coat.

"You work for Tate?"

"I don't."

The man studied him a second longer before turning back to the boy he still held pinned under his bear paw of a hand. "This kid took my Bowie. I set it down inside. He was the only one in there." He must have squeezed the boy's throat because the kid let out a squeak.

"You take the man's knife?" James asked the boy.

The kid shook his head under the too-large hat he wore.

"How about you turn out your pockets to satisfy Mister . . ." James looked to the big man to fill in his name.

"Ayers. This is my place of business."

Judging from how drunk the man was, James was glad he wasn't leaving his horse here overnight. He nodded at the kid. "Turn out your pockets."

The boy immediately reached down and pulled out the pockets sewn into his coat. They were empty.

But the bigger man didn't let go. "How's I know he didn't stick it down in his boot? Or in his trousers?"

James doubted the poor kid would do a whole lot of stealing after this, provided he even took the knife to begin with. More than likely, the man had kicked it under some straw. "I'll tell you what. Suppose you just buy yourself a new one? If this kid took it, he probably needs it." He gave a side glance at the boy, who now, upon closer inspection, looked familiar. James couldn't quite place it, though. He pulled a few bills from his pocket and handed them out to the man. "It's all I've got, but should be more than enough to get you an even better knife."

The man wrapped his meaty hand around the money and tucked it into his pocket, grinning at James. "This here is good service. You oughta put Tate out of business. Take over. I like your kind."

"I appreciate that. Now how about you let the kid go?"

The boy's face was turning a shade of red James could see even in the dim light that shone from the battered lamp hanging nearby.

"Right." The man glared at the boy before spitting onto the ground and drawing his hand away. "Good for nothing kid," he muttered as he stumbled back into the building.

The boy had already started off without a word, slinking down the side of the building toward the darkness beyond when James took a few long steps and grabbed hold of his arm. "I wasn't done with you yet."

The kid came to a quick halt, letting out a high-pitched squeak when James's hand closed around his arm. Higher pitched than a boy this age ought to have. And the familiarity . . . It was the eyes, and the shape of the chin . . .

James drew the kid around to face him. It couldn't be.

He plucked the hat from the boy's head, and a long copper-brown braid tumbled out.

Miss Dutton.

Chapter Fourteen

Edie froze as Deputy Wright uttered her name. He wasn't supposed to know she was here. No one was. Her mind churned as she searched for a way to explain her presence in the camp. Up this close, she could see him without her spectacles on, and his eyes swept up and down her trousers and shirt-covered form. She wore her usual coat unbuttoned, thinking it was plain enough to pass for a boy's coat, but under no circumstances could she have a believable explanation for wearing men's clothes that she'd filched from the hotel laundry.

At least it was dark this far down, and he couldn't see the bright flush she felt sure covered her cheeks at being caught in such a state. The last time she'd worn such clothes was years ago, back when Pa would take her out hunting with her brothers. She hadn't thought twice about it then, especially since she'd only been with her family, but out here, on a public street, clad only in trousers, a shirt, and a coat, she felt almost naked.

"I don't know where to start," Deputy Wright said, his hand still on her arm.

"How about you begin with letting my arm go?"

He glanced at his hand, almost as if he'd forgotten he was holding her. He released her arm, and she hurriedly buttoned her coat, feeling at least halfway decent now that it was closed. She pulled her glasses from a pocket sewn into the trousers and replaced them on her nose.

"I'm sure you're wondering why I'm here," she said, still not entirely settled on what she'd tell him but figuring it best to offer the explanation herself rather than wait for him to ask.

"That, and why you're dressed in . . ." He waved a hand at her clothing. "What possessed you to come to such a place?"

She pushed her shoulders back and held out her hand for the hat she'd worn. The deputy returned it silently, presumably still waiting for her answer. She took her time tucking the braid back underneath it. "That is precisely why I'm wearing men's clothing. I hoped not to draw attention to myself. Of course, I didn't plan for the livery owner to think I stole his knife."

A couple of men strode across the yard of the livery, and they were both quiet until the men had passed.

"You can tell me the rest when we're on our way," he said under his breath, even though there was no one around to overhear.

"I can't leave. I haven't accomplished what I came to do." Edie crossed her arms. She didn't sneak out of her room without waking Beatrice, take clothes that didn't belong to her, and ride all the way out here only to be ordered back.

"You will leave. Or I'll tie you to your horse." James's voice was low, almost a growl.

She took a step back from him. He was absolutely serious. He hadn't struck her as the sort of man to be so demanding, and yet here he was, insisting on his way just like every other man she'd ever known.

He softened some and reached for her hand. "Look," he said. "I've been around this camp tonight. Anything you want to know is likely something I already know. And if I don't, I can return and find out for you. But right now, you need to get out of here. I'll see you home."

Edie glanced down at her hand in his. It made her feel as if nothing in the world could ever harm her, just as it had when he'd taken her hand in the wagon on the way to Cañon City.

She pondered her options. It had been no small undertaking to get here, but she didn't much relish the idea of wandering into a saloon, hoping to catch wind of the names of the men who'd caused trouble the other night. And she especially feared the possibility that, if it were her family, some of them might still be here, ready to spot her even through her disguise. "All right. If I can hold you to your word."

"I don't take promises lightly. Wait here, in the shadows. I'll return with the horses."

Edie did as he said. She shoved both hands into the pockets of her coat, trying to forget the feel of his fingers around hers. She needed to concentrate, to figure out a way she could get the information she needed without giving too much away. If Deputy Wright ever found out she was related to the Beaumonts . . .

She shivered in the night air, imagining the look of disgust that would cross his face. She didn't think she could bear it. Even if everything pointed against her growing any closer to him, she never wanted him to think any less of her.

He returned with the horses saddled. "Would you believe Mr. Ayers is fast asleep in a pile of straw?"

Edie grinned in spite of herself. "I do believe it." He held out cupped hands for her to step into. It was a sweet, thoughtful gesture, and one she didn't need at all. Instead, she gripped the saddle horn and swung herself up, leaving Deputy Wright looking at her in equal amounts of curiosity and awe. To his credit, he neither remarked on that or on the fact that she sat astride.

"I grew up on horses," she said. "As soon as I was strong enough, I could get myself into the saddle."

He stood up straight and caught his own horse's reins. "You had a more interesting childhood than I imagine most ladies do, Miss Dutton," he said.

Edie was thankful that he rode out in front of her at that moment, because the look on her face might have betrayed her. "I suppose I have," she said quietly.

They said nothing more as they rode through the camp. Edie searched the passing miners for any familiar faces. Deputy Wright, she supposed, scanned the same faces for potential trouble.

Once the camp was far behind them, he slowed his horse to allow Edie to pull up alongside. "Now, are you going to tell me what brings an otherwise upstanding Gilbert Girl out to a mining camp after curfew?"

Edie bit her lip. He must have spoken with Mr. McFarland to know about the rules the waitresses lived by. Although if he had, he'd also know she'd lose her position if either the McFarlands or Mrs. Ruby learned they'd spent any time together, alone.

"Edie?" he prodded, his voice as smooth as the dark, clouded sky above them.

Edie shifted the reins in her hands, trying not to think on how he'd just used her given name. As if he knew her well. As if they were something more than just a sheriff's deputy and a lost woman. She hadn't told him her name. He must have learned it from someone else, which meant he'd been speaking about her to . . . whom? And why would he be talking about her? Her heart thumped hard as she considered the possibilities. Clearly he hadn't learned anything about her thefts from the hotel or Mr. Adkins, or else she doubted he'd be speaking to her.

"You don't need to fear telling me anything," he said.

She looked up at him, expecting to see that same look of pity others often wore. But it wasn't there. All that looked back at her was an open, kind, and decidedly handsome face. It was as if he thought her something special, something more than Jonas Beaumont's daughter, something better than the girl who'd stolen from the hotel. It was disconcerting. His eyes held hers until she thought she'd forgotten how to breathe.

"I'm not who you think I am," she finally said, her voice barely audible over the quiet breeze and the crickets' song.

"What do you mean?"

What had she said? Edie squeezed her eyes shut and concentrated on the back and forth motion of the horse beneath her. What had possessed her to say such a thing?

When she opened her eyes and glanced over at him, he wore a kind but serious expression. He wanted an answer, and she couldn't dance around it. As close to the truth as she could get seemed again the best way forward.

Edie buried her chin in her coat as she spoke. "Only that I don't always make the best decisions." She pushed forward in the hopes that he'd forget she hadn't thoroughly answered his question. "I'd heard word that one of my brothers might have just arrived in camp. If he's there, I wanted to see him. I miss my brothers dearly."

"What is his name?"

Name. Thinking quickly, she blurted out, "Tyrone Dutton." It was, perhaps, a little too close to the truth, but surely there were many men named Tyrone. And she hadn't used his nickname.

"I can't say I've heard word of a man by that name, but I'll ask around."

"I'm grateful." He wouldn't ever find a man by such a name—not that she'd want her brother to know where she was, as much as she did miss him—but the kindness of Deputy Wright's offer touched her heart. "I—"

Deputy Wright drew up short. "Stop," he said, a finger against his lips.

She did as he said, halting her horse while raising her eyebrows in question. But he said nothing else as he turned around to face the direction from which they'd come.

And then she heard it. Off in the distance, likely toward the camp though it was hard to tell out here in the valley, came the unmistakable sound of hooves pounding the ground.

Had someone followed them? It might be that livery owner, awake and angry that she'd gotten away. Or worse, someone she'd actually been searching for.

She needed to go. *Now*. Before whoever the person was caught up with them. Just as she was about to nudge her horse into motion, Deputy Wright rode into her line of vision. He pointed silently to the north, where an expanse of trees guarded what was likely a small water source.

Breathing so hard she thought for certain the man on the horse a distance away could hear her, Edie followed Deputy Wright to the trees. As soon as they were hidden from view, he dismounted and tied his horse to a tree. Edie followed suit and then scurried after him back up to the last few trees that sat back from the path between Crest Stone and the mining camp. The moment the man came into view on the far left, Deputy Wright drew a revolver from his hip with his right hand. With his free hand, he pressed her back behind him.

She tried to peer over his shoulder and finally settled on looking around him. His strong arm held her back, his fingers wrapped around her wrist, as he tracked the man and his horse across what felt like the width of the entire valley. Even when the man was out of sight, he stayed poised just like that for a few moments longer before finally lowering his gun and letting go of her arm.

She shivered in the cool air, wrapping her arms around herself while he stepped out beyond the trees. When he returned, he stopped in front of her. His face was impassive, but something in the air felt different. Edie hugged her arms tighter around herself.

"I'm curious about something," he finally said. "One thing that doesn't quite make sense."

Her mind raced. Had she misspoken at some point? Had she given too much away? All of these falsehoods made her head spin. Her fingers dug into her arms, and she wondered if she might tell him everything. Perhaps being truthful wouldn't be so terrible.

The temptation was so strong it almost made her forget why she'd kept so much from him to begin with.

He took a step forward, his eyes narrowed.

She gulped, holding the words back with all her might. She had to be certain.

"Edie?" he pressed.

Chapter Fifteen

Miss Dutton's eyes widened as James took another step forward. What had he said that made her look so terrified? "I'm only curious about how you got that horse," he said. "How did you sneak it out without the stable hands knowing?"

"Oh," she said, a nervous laugh following the word. "I can be very convincing when I want to be. After all, I had five brothers I was forever trying to get things from back home. Food usually works."

The very image of this wisp of a girl trading a pie for a horse made him laugh. "Food does work," he conceded. "I should know. My sisters got more out of me that way than anything else. My youngest sister, Emily, used to bribe me with okra."

"Okra?" Edie wrinkled her nose.

James smiled to himself. He shouldn't think of her as Edie, but the name fit her so much better than Miss Dutton. "Yes, okra. Fried okra, spicy."

"Are you teasing me?" She lifted her chin as if she didn't quite believe him.

"I'm serious as a cyclone. You've never had spicy fried okra?"

"I have . . ." She trailed off, evidently still puzzled.

"It's my favorite food."

"It is not."

"It is. Emily could get anything she wanted out of me with a plate of spicy fried okra."

And that was when Edie burst out laughing, all trace of whatever had unnerved her earlier gone. Her laugh was sweet, warm and yet a bit garbled, almost as if she hadn't laughed in ages. And come to think of it, he hadn't seen her laugh at all before.

It was as if she'd let something loose, just for him. Unbidden, he raised a hand and rested his fingers on her cheek. He'd taken off his gloves when he'd pulled the revolver, and now his fingers made contact with the soft skin on her face.

Edie's eyes fluttered shut and she went still. Her face was so perfect, seemingly carved from porcelain and yet soft and warm to the touch. Wisps of her hair framed her forehead under the ridiculous hat she wore. He lifted it from her head, and her hair fell in its braid down her back. "You are the most beautiful woman I've ever met."

Her eyes blinked open, and she looked up at him, disbelieving.

The words were out now, and he couldn't take them back. And in fact, he didn't want to take them back. If Edie was a distraction, all he wanted in this moment was to be distracted for the rest of his life.

"I don't believe you, Deputy Wright," she said, those soft brown eyes searching his face for the truth.

"James."

"James," she repeated. "I'm plain enough to have the sense to not believe an outright falsehood such as that."

"If you're plain, then I suppose I find that beautiful. But believe me, Edie Dutton, you are not plain." He traced her cheek with his thumb. More than anything, he wanted to drop that hat to the ground and use his other hand to guide her toward him.

Her lips parted, almost as if she was thinking the same thing. He tightened his grip on the hat brim, fighting the desire to touch his lips to hers.

Behind her a horse snuffled, and then, out of nowhere, a velvety muzzle nudged against the hand that rested on her cheek.

Edie jumped, and James yanked his hand away. Edie's horse stood right there, no longer tied to the tree several feet behind them. The horse snuffled again and stepped forward, searching for attention.

James glanced at Edie. A smile danced on her lips until she caught his eye. Then they both burst into laughter at the same time. Edie reached out and scratched the horse's nose. "I suppose I didn't pay enough attention to knotting the reins about that tree," she said as soon as she caught her breath.

"That rider should be far enough ahead of us that we can head back now," James said, although he'd be keeping a close eye on their surroundings the entire way. It was likely nothing, just one of the men on one of the building crews or a hotel employee returning from a night of gambling or drinking. But he knew better than to let his guard down.

They mounted their horses, and yet again, James was struck with Edie's strength. How a woman her size had the strength to pull herself up into the saddle like that both puzzled and amazed him. Even his sister Tilly, the one who adored horses, used a stool to get into the saddle. And Tilly hadn't ridden astride since she was a young girl. Yet it seemed it didn't even occur to Edie not to.

She loved books, could brew up a tea to cure headaches, rode a horse as if she were born on one, had no idea how beautiful she was, and seemed entirely fine with wearing men's clothing.

Edie Dutton was unlike any woman he'd ever met.

Perhaps he'd been wrong all these years. He was certain he'd never be married if he pursued a career as a lawman, not after what had happened to his uncle. But other men seemed to have both. Sheriff Young had managed to keep order in his work and still marry.

Maybe such a life was possible for him, too. He pondered the idea as he led the way out of the trees and back toward Crest Stone.

In fact, he wasn't certain he could imagine his life without Edie in it.

Chapter Sixteen

"Edie! Will you hurry along?" Millie swung the basket of food as she turned to wait, her red hair peeking out from under the wide-brimmed straw hat she wore.

Edie shook her head to clear it. She'd been walking through what felt like a dream all morning, and now, as she hurried to catch up to Millie, Dora, and Emma, she wondered if she'd ever wake up from it.

Or whether she even wanted to.

"It's a man, isn't it?" Millie eyed her as they tagged along behind the other girls. Her eyes widened. "Wait! It's the fellow who works with the sheriff. Deputy Wright, the one who was fairly mooning over you in Cañon City. I'm right, aren't I?"

Edie huffed, but she had to look away as a smile took over her face. "How would you know about that? If I recall, you had to work that day."

"Not a whisper of gossip escapes me, you know that. Now, tell me all about him."

Edie pressed her lips shut. Millie was the last person who needed to know.

"I'm actually quite good at keeping confidences, when I'm directed to." Millie smiled at her. "Let's see, you could ask Penny, or Dora, or—"

"All right, I believe you," Edie said. "But that doesn't mean there's anything to tell."

"Hmm. We'll see about that. Why, I believe that's your lawman just up ahead, helping out with the building." Millie pointed, and Edie followed her finger.

And sure enough, there, just past the barn behind the general store, was Deputy Wright. Or James, she thought, her cheeks warming at the memory of him insisting she call him by his Christian name as his hand rested on her face.

"Why, Emma, it almost looks fit enough to live in!" Millie teased as she set down the basket.

Emma laughed as her husband came forward to embrace her. A couple other men who'd been working on the house paused also. Edie recognized Dora's husband, Mr. Gilbert, and the proprietor of the general store, Mr. Drexel. And, of course, James.

He stood watching her now, a smile alighting his lips when she caught his eye. With everyone else otherwise engaged, it felt as if they were alone.

"Mr. Hartley," Dora was saying. "Are you going to see Elizabeth any time soon? If you are, could you pass along a gift from me?"

"I'd be delighted, Mrs. Gilbert," Mr. Hartley said, an arm still wrapped around Emma's waist.

Edie remembered Mr. Hartley's sister, who'd arrived at the hotel just before Christmas. She hadn't worked there long before she married a cowboy and moved with him to a ranch somewhere northeast of Crest Stone.

"I suppose you'll be building me a house next?" Millie said as she scrutinized the men's work. "I prefer a two-story in the Colonial style."

The girls laughed while Edie smiled. It was so rare for her to laugh, and the fact that she didn't now only served to remind her of when she did laugh with Deputy Wright—James—last night. She was so caught up in her thoughts again that she almost missed Dora's quiet announcement.

"I believe they may be building Jake and me a house next," she said.

Everyone looked at Mr. Gilbert for confirmation. "The railroad asked if I would run the land office, once it's built," he said, taking Dora's hand. "It will be temporary, considering I'd prefer to start my own business."

"I think it's a wonderful opportunity," Dora said, her face tilted up to smile at her husband.

The men congratulated him, while the ladies began discussing where Dora might have her home built. Edie hung back, watching the easy way that Mr. Gilbert kept his arm around his wife, and the adoring manner in which she watched him as he spoke. Her eyes instinctively flitted to James.

He stood behind the other men, a hand propped on one of the wooden beams of the Hartleys' home. He watched the happy couple with a smile, but when his gaze turned to Edie, he grew more serious. He nodded his head ever so slightly toward the barn that sat between them and the mercantile, and then ambled away in that direction.

Edie's heart picked up pace. No one noticed that James had disappeared. Everyone was so absorbed in discussions of building and furnishing houses, and all eyes were on Dora and her husband. Edie hesitated a few moments, and then, sending up a little prayer that none of the girls would notice her absence for at least a few minutes, picked up her skirts and quietly moved toward the barn.

James stood waiting on the far side of the building, which faced the rear of the mercantile. The sun was nearly directly overhead, casting barely a shadow but warming the day up quite well. James had already shed his coat at the building site, and Edie had left hers back at the hotel, opting instead for a shawl. It was so nice to be outside without a coat. She'd almost forgotten what it felt like.

She stopped a couple feet away from James, suddenly bashful. Perhaps she'd imagined the meanings behind his actions last night. After all, he'd saved her from that terrible man at the livery, and then they'd had to hide from the stranger on the horse. It was possible that everything he did was only to keep her safe.

But even as she had the thoughts, she knew they weren't entirely true. And as if to reassure her of that fact, James held out a hand. She stepped forward and took it, his palm warm through the thin cotton of her glove. He held up her hand and inspected the glove.

"I don't see how anything that thin could keep your hands warm," he said.

A smile teased up the corners of her mouth. "They aren't meant for warmth."

He raised his eyebrows.

"They're to prevent freckles. Although I fear I may be too late in wearing them, considering I was never too diligent about it as a girl."

"Are you telling me you have freckled hands?" He was on the verge of laughter, and Edie grinned.

"I may have a few."

"Hmm." He took hold of her other hand and pulled her closer toward him. "I'm not certain I can court a woman with freckled hands."

Edie felt as if a rock had lodged itself in her throat. "Are you—is that—" She couldn't finish a sentence.

That only made him smile more. He pulled one of his hands from hers only to push a lock of her hair back with it. "Would you like that?"

She blinked at him. It was the absolute last thing she'd expected. And—her heart sank—the one thing that couldn't happen. "James."

His face seemed to light up when she said his name. The same stubborn curl of hair had fallen forward again, and he pushed it back, letting his hand linger on the side of her face, just as he had last night. "I know it's not allowed, not while you're under contract with the Gilbert Company. Yet I wonder how your friends came to be married?"

Edie lifted a hand and closed it over his. She couldn't think straight with his fingers tracing her jaw as they were. "They met in secret. It happened before I arrived, but I heard that Emma—Mrs. Hartley—was found out and dismissed." She saw the way he smiled at her, hope tracing every feature on his face. She wanted so badly to meet that hope, to reassure him she desired this as much as he did. But the risk was too great. If she lost her position and things did not work out between the two of them . . . And then, of course, there was the small matter of her family. "James, I can't do that. Please don't ask me to."

"I wouldn't. We can wait until your contract is fulfilled in the fall. But of course we'll happen to run into each other in the meantime." He grinned at her, and she couldn't help but return it. "What do you think?"

Fall. She should know by then if he was worth the risk of her not renewing her contract with the hotel. The back of her mind buzzed with every other reason she shouldn't agree to such an arrangement. Would she continue with her false name? Could she keep the secret of her family for . . . how long? Forever? The disruption in the camp had only been miners, he'd told her last night. There was no new evidence that her family was anywhere near here, or that they knew where she was. But what if they were out there, somewhere, biding their time?

Even as his strong hand held hers, her other hand clenched as she fought to push those worries aside. She shook it out and raised it, brushing her fingers across his forehead. "How are your headaches?"

"Manageable, thanks to your herbs. You work miracles, Edie." He caught her hand in his. "You didn't answer my question."

"I . . ." She raised her eyes to his face. He smiled at her, and there was nothing hidden in the depths of his eyes. She suddenly wished he would kiss her.

It was a wild thought, and she didn't quite know where it had come from, but now it was all she could think about. Visions of a future with him burst into her mind, burying any thought of her family. "I think . . . that might be all right."

His grin broadened and he closed the distance between them. He raised a hand and lifted her chin. Edie could hardly breathe. Everything around them disappeared—the talk from her friends on the other side of the barn, the hammering from one of the other building sites, the clanging from the blacksmith's shop, even the birdsong. It all disappeared and only James existed. Edie's eyes closed, and his breath warmed her face. All she wanted to do was wrap her arms around his neck and pull him down toward her, but she remained still, waiting. Just as his lips touched hers, her name sounded from somewhere around the barn, breaking the stillness that had otherwise settled around them.

"Edie? We're going to eat. Where are you?" Millie's voice called.

James leapt backward. Edie placed her hands flat against the barn behind her. Somehow, now that he was separated from her, she felt as if she couldn't hold herself up.

He reached out, touched her face, and mouthed, *Later.* And then he was gone, disappeared around the far side of the barn just as Millie strode around from the nearer corner.

"What are you doing back here?" Millie's face scrunched up as she looked around the yard between the barn and the mercantile. Her eyes landed on the mercantile, which had housed the very first Gilbert Girls to arrive before the hotel was built. "Oh, I don't miss living here at all. We slept four to a room. And we had to cook and wash the laundry and fetch water. Can you imagine?"

While Millie talked, Edie straightened and attempted to pull her mind away from James. They'd come so close to being caught, and yet all Edie could think about was how he'd been about to kiss her. What was wrong with her? She could have laughed with the absurdity of it all.

Millie had stopped speaking and was watching Edie expectantly, as if waiting for an answer.

"Oh, I . . ." She trailed off, searching for a good explanation.

"You know, I suspected you'd run off with that handsome lawman, only he isn't here." Millie gave her a sly grin. "Which only means you came to use the privy."

"Yes," Edie said, only now registering the existence of such a thing in the yard nearby.

"Well, let's go eat. I believe Dora packed us all sorts of good things." Millie took Edie by the elbow and chattered on.

Edie tried valiantly to pay attention, and yet, when they rounded the barn, all she could see was James, standing with the other men, and talking as if nothing had happened.

One of the other girls had spread a couple of quilts on the ground, and everyone sat to partake of the food Dora had prepared. The conversation moved from the food to the upcoming summer and speculation on what other newcomers the growing town might bring. Edie snuck looks at James only to find him doing the same.

Edie smiled to herself as she sat back, leaning her weight on her hands. The blue sky stretched on for miles above, meeting snowcapped mountains that glistened in the sunlight. A warm breeze lifted the strands of her hair that had fallen from the hasty chignon she'd done earlier. And she realized she'd never felt so content.

Her family felt hundreds of miles away, where they belonged. She was safe here in this valley, with friends she'd never imagined she'd ever have, and now a wonderful man who seemed to care for her as much as she cared for him. It was so unlikely that the men making trouble east of here were Beaumonts. And even if it was her family, they'd have no reason to know she was here. Mr. Adkins wouldn't want her pa to know where he was now, considering he thought she'd told her pa everything he'd done.

Perhaps she could live the rest of her life here in this beautiful place as Edie Dutton, or, if she dared hope, Edie Wright. She almost giggled at the thought. It was a strange sensation, feeling the desire to laugh so frequently. Here she was, seemingly without a care in the world, tittering over a handsome man who promised to court her. She needn't ever tell him about her family. They wouldn't come here. If she pressed the secret down far enough, perhaps she could forget about it too.

She glanced back at him again, only to find him watching her with a peaceful smile.

Maybe being Edie Wright wasn't too far out of the realm of possibility after all.

Chapter Seventeen

Days passed in a flurry of meeting new people, talking with those James had already met, helping Hartley with his house, and catching fleeting moments with Edie at the hotel restaurant. After having nearly been caught by Edie's red-haired friend, James didn't dare try to catch her alone again. It was no use getting her into trouble with the hotel, and he'd never forgive himself if he ruined her reputation. Besides, he needed to busy himself with his work. Now that he knew she felt the same way about him, there would be plenty of time to court her when she was free of her contract.

If only it weren't so hard to wait.

It didn't matter what he did, she was always in his thoughts. She was the first person he searched for when he entered a room, and the first image in his head when he woke in the morning. At this rate, he didn't know how he'd last the four months or so before her contract ended.

He'd just finished helping Hartley for the day and was making his way slowly back to the hotel when the depot clerk's young helper came running down the tracks as if the devil himself were chasing the boy.

"Deputy Wright!" Christopher shouted.

"Have I another telegram?" James hadn't received news from Sheriff Young in a few days. While he supposed no news was good news, he was on the verge of telegraphing his boss himself to find out for certain.

"No, sir." The boy stopped and fell into step next to James. "There's a fella at the depot. He just rode in from a ranch, looking for you."

"Did he give a name?" James knew some of the valley's ranchers, from when they'd come up to Cañon City for goods or to deliver cattle to the rail yard.

"No, sir. He's waiting for you."

"Then let's go see what he wants." It couldn't be good, if it caused the man to ride all the way here.

74

A tall dark-haired man waited near a horse outside the depot. Christopher ran ahead and offered to take the man's horse up to the hotel's stables. The man declined and then looked toward James.

James held out a hand. "James Wright. I hear you're looking for me?"

The man shook his hand. He had an intense and serious manner about him, one that indicated he had no patience for anything that stood in his way. "Isaac Trenton. I own the Aspen Ridge ranch up north of here. I had some horses stolen last night. Five to be exact. I attempted to follow the trail, but they were careful. From what I could tell, they headed southeast."

"Toward the camp," James said, thinking out loud.

"I can protect my own," Trenton said, looking off into the distance. "But I thought you might know who it was."

James rubbed a hand over the short beard that now covered his chin. "I have a few ideas. I'll ride out there and see what I find."

Trenton thanked him and rode off. Before James made his way up to the hotel to gather what he needed, he sent Ben a telegram. It was possible the thieves had changed direction and headed north to Cañon City. And if they had, it would be a lot harder to track down Trenton's horses in a town of that size.

Telegram sent, he moved quickly back up to the hotel to gather supplies for the ride, a set of the wanted posters to give to Marshal Tate that he should have brought on his last ride to the camp, and another borrowed horse. He was halfway down the hill from the hotel when he realized he needed to eat. Working through meals sometimes brought on the headaches, and that was the last thing he could afford to deal with right now. He should've brewed some of the tea Edie had given him as a precaution before he left, but he didn't want to spare the time. Instead of returning to the hotel, he tied up his horse outside the mercantile. Mrs. Drexel usually had some sort of baked good to sell. That would do to tide him over and keep the headaches at bay.

Inside, the little store was a flurry of activity. A couple of men James recognized from building crews were at the counter, another rancher was talking with Mr. Drexel about seed, and a handful of girls in gray and white dresses perused the items on the shelves. James had taken only a couple of steps toward the counter and the glass stand that held a mouthwatering coffee cake, when one person in particular caught his eye.

Edie. There she was, standing alone near one of the front windows, admiring a small selection of pottery. James's eyes flitted between her and the coffee cake. He should get going, purchase something to eat and then head out to the mining camp, but his eyes kept coming back to Edie. She'd picked up a small vessel with a little lid and smiled at it as if its mere presence in the store was enough to make her entire day. Just watching her drew a smile to James's face. He waited until she'd set the little jar down before joining her.

"Do you have a need for jars and . . ." He inclined his head toward the pottery, not entirely knowing what to call the selection on the shelves.

She tilted her head up to him, and the most beautiful smile he'd ever seen crossed her face. It was as if she lit up just because he was here. It warmed him up from the inside and made him feel as if he could accomplish anything, just because this woman was happy to see him.

"Mrs. McFarland says I might plant a small garden behind the hotel. I'll need a few little containers like this in which to keep the herbs and plants I harvest." She eyed his coat and the saddlebags slung over his shoulder. "You look prepared for a journey."

"I'm riding back out to the camp. Some horses went missing last night from a ranch nearby, and the tracks point eastward." He shifted the saddlebags, reminded of the need to get moving.

Edie's eyes had gone wide at the information. "Is it . . ."

"There's nothing indicating it's either of the Kansas gangs," he said, anticipating her question. "Most likely it's only a couple of drifters, looking to make a bit of money before they head elsewhere." He gave her a reassuring smile. "Most of those miners can't afford horses. If the thieves went to the camp, they shouldn't be hard to track down."

She smiled, but the light had gone from her eyes. James glanced about the store, but they were fairly well hidden up here at the front, behind the shelf with the pottery. He took her hand and squeezed it. "You have no need to fear."

Edie looked up at him. "Thank you." She held his gaze, but he could tell she wasn't entirely convinced. Something had her worried, distracted.

"Listen to me." He held her hand close and waited until her eyes locked with his. "I promise you that if the Fletchers or Beaumonts find their way to this valley, I *will* track them down."

She nodded.

"I spent the better part of a year after the Fletchers before I left home. The last thing I want is to have them here."

Her head tilted, and he could see the question in her eyes, but his uncle's death wasn't exactly something he wanted to revisit at this moment, not in the mercantile, and not when he needed his head on straight to deal with these horse thieves. "Do you trust me?" he asked her.

"I do," she said, but there was still something there, some faraway doubt he couldn't quite capture, even when she smiled at him. It was haunted, as if she were also protecting some broken part of her. Perhaps they'd touched her family too, in some way. He'd ask her later, when they had more time to talk. But now, he needed to get moving.

"I must go. I'll see you again soon." And, after checking to ensure no one was looking, he leaned forward and gave her a quick kiss on the cheek. It wasn't enough—nothing ever was—but it had to be for now.

Her face instantly colored and a hand drifted up to where he'd kissed her. She gave him a shy smile, and with that lovely picture in his mind, he purchased a couple slices of coffee cake, left the store, and turned his horse eastward.

Images of Edie danced through his mind while he rode, so much so that he had to force them away. He needed to keep his attention on his surroundings, else he might find himself taken by surprise. But as her sweet voice and the endearing way she'd blushed when he kissed her entered his mind again and again, drawing his focus away from the reason he was out here at all, the old fears returned.

Was she too much of a distraction? He couldn't afford to ride into the camp with his mind wandering in such a way.

No, she wasn't, he was certain of that. How could something that felt so right be nothing but a distraction? Except, it seemed impossible for him to remain focused on work. And in his line of work, that could be deadly.

But somehow Ben had succeeded in having a wife. A lot of lawmen did. And yet his uncle had died because of a woman.

No, he hadn't died because he'd fallen in love. It happened because Uncle Mark had fallen for the wrong woman, and she'd turned his head from any instinct he might have felt that something wasn't right. James's situation wasn't the same, not at all. Edie was a good, honest woman.

So long as he kept his wits about him while he was working, this would all turn out exactly as he wished.

Chapter Eighteen

E die hung back as Beatrice and Sarah left the store. They waited for her just outside, and she couldn't remain here forever, despite how much James's news had unnerved her. So she pulled in a deep breath, told herself she was being overly cautious, and exited.

Thankfully, her friends were too busy discussing Sarah's purchases to notice anything about Edie. She remained behind them as they picked their way around the mud that had been churned up along the makeshift road. She found herself searching every person they passed for a familiar face. By the time they crossed the tracks, the sense of dread that had settled into her stomach back at the store had lightened only a little.

Stealing horses was her family's quickest way to make money in between bigger jobs. If they'd run low on flour or one of the boys needed new shoes and it had been a while since the last job, Pa and Cousin Nick would filch a horse or two. And worst of all, Edie never realized it was such a terrible thing until she was nearly grown. The memory made her cheeks color now, even though she knew it wasn't her fault. It was impossible to understand right from wrong when your family made all their wrongs seem right.

But now she knew. And she would never go back to that sort of life.

"You're awfully quiet. Are you all right?" Sarah asked as they passed the depot.

Edie tried her best to give her friends a reassuring smile. "It's nothing. Only lost in thought."

Beatrice shot Sarah a knowing grin. Normally, Edie would have insisted her thoughts had nothing to do with James, but she was far too preoccupied now. It was a wonder that every girl in the hotel seemed to know of James's fondness for her, and yet managed to keep it secret from Mrs. Ruby.

When her friends returned to their conversation, Edie's mind fell to James and his ride out to the camp. She shuddered at the thought of that place. It was, however, the perfect location for her family to hide in plain sight. And if they were desperate for cash, a good place to sell off some horses for cheap. What if James found them?

It was as if the sun had disappeared entirely. A chill crept through her body, and Edie hugged her arms to herself tightly. As much as she wanted nothing to do with them again, the idea of Pa or Nick or Ty or any of her other brothers awaiting a noose from inside a cell made her feel sick. And what would happen if James cornered them? They wouldn't go easily. Her family avoided bloodshed, but they wouldn't shy from it if there was no other way out.

She wanted to drop down onto her knees right there on the sage-covered hill that led up to the hotel and pray as if she'd never prayed before. But she couldn't, not right now, not without her friends thinking she'd lost her mind. So she settled for repeating a fervent prayer in her head, over and over. James could not find her family. It wouldn't end well for either side.

When they reached the kitchen door on the side of the hotel, Edie pled enjoyment of the fresh air to remain outside a few moments longer. Beatrice gave her a concerned look, but Edie smiled at her, and finally, her roommate followed Sarah inside. Edie returned to the front corner of the hotel and leaned against the wooden wall, the beginnings of the town spread out before her just down the hill.

It might not be her family at all. It could be the Fletchers. It could be some wayward horse thieves. Oh, how she hoped it was the latter. But if it wasn't . . .

Edie steadied her breathing as she watched the men moving to and fro on each side of the tracks, raising wood, cutting logs, hammering. New men arrived and left each day. At least inside the hotel, she only saw those who could afford a meal or lodging for the night. Down the hill . . . anyone might see her.

She could keep to the hotel. With her false surname, she was hidden here. None of her family would ever venture inside.

Unless they already knew she was here.

Although even as that thought crossed her mind, Edie frowned. The worry was always there, and thanks to Mr. Adkins, it would likely never go away.

Could she live like this for the rest of her life?

Did she have a choice?

She didn't know, but the alternative would mean leaving Crest Stone, the only place she'd ever felt as if she truly belonged. It would mean leaving James.

No, she'd remain. She would be smart and stay near the hotel, keeping vigilant watch. And if her family knew she was here, surely she'd hear about them arriving in the town below before they got to the hotel. She'd have time to figure something out.

And she'd continue praying that James wouldn't meet up with Pa or Nick or her brothers. Because if anything happened to him at their hands, she would never forgive herself.

Chapter Nineteen

" Tall, you said, but fair?" James rubbed at his chin. He was getting nowhere with these people.

"And one of them had a scarred-up face," the miner added, his friend nodding vigorously in agreement. They'd already pocketed the money James had given them to buy the two horses back.

"One looked like a kid," the friend said.

Considering the other two men who'd bought the stolen horses had described "a bunch of old men" and "maybe an Indian," James didn't think he was any closer at all to identifying the thieves. The men were likely long gone from the camp by this point, anyhow.

James thanked them and led the horses through the growing darkness to the livery, where the three other stolen animals had already been turned out in the corral. He'd send word to Mr. Trenton to come get them as soon as he returned to Crest Stone. He paid the only slightly more sober Mr. Ayers for their care, and saddled his own borrowed horse to return to the hotel.

On his way out, he spoke with the camp marshal again to relay what he'd learned and give him a set of the wanted posters. The man had only been too happy to have James do his work for him in tracking down the stolen horses, and didn't seem too inclined to care much about the goings on outside his camp.

James rode out just as the night was beginning, and he was happy to leave the place in his dust. He only hoped the livery owner could be trusted not to sell off Trenton's horses a second time before the man could arrive to claim them.

He pulled the last bit of coffee cake from his saddlebags and polished it off as he rode. What he'd do for some homemade cake on a regular basis. The little place in Cañon City where he usually ate had decent meals, but didn't do much in the way of baking. He wondered if Edie cared for baking. It didn't much matter if she did, but if he were being honest, he hoped she enjoyed it.

A horse nickered from somewhere behind him.

James stiffened. How had he—

A shot rang out.

His horse reared up. Unprepared, James flew from the saddle, landing hard on his left side. Another shot cracked the night around him. He reached for one of his pistols and stayed low to the ground, searching the shadows around him for anything that might indicate who was shooting at him.

The crescent moon barely provided any light, and he couldn't see very far past his immediate surroundings. His heart thudded and every sense felt magnified. It was quiet for a few moments. All he could hear was his own breath and the sounds of his horse, which—thankfully—hadn't run very far.

He rose slowly, turning to survey the land around him as best he could, with the revolver outstretched in front of him.

Then, out of nowhere, a sharp pain shot through the back of his head. The last he knew, the ground was rising to meet him.

WHEN JAMES OPENED HIS eyes, it wasn't to see the papered walls of his room at the Crest Stone Hotel. Instead, it was to a faceful of sage and a night filled with twinkling stars. Confused for half a second, he remained where he was, and then it slowly returned. The sound of a horse, the gunshot, the strike on the back of his head.

Common sense told him to remain still and listen, and so he did. When he heard nothing but the usual sounds of night, he lifted a hand and gingerly felt along the back of his scalp. A tender bump had already begun to swell.

James sat up slowly. His head pounded, but in a much different way than when he was stricken with the headaches. Remarkably, whoever had come after him had left him alive. But if they hadn't killed him, what did they want? To scare him?

He hauled himself to his feet, his head protesting the entire way. The horse still stood nearby, chewing contentedly on some grass, seemingly unconcerned that someone had knocked his master unconscious. The beast was nothing like

James's own Tartan, who he liked to think would have at least attempted to nudge him awake. Or charged after the man who'd done this.

He made his way toward the horse, and that was when he found what the man—or men—had been after.

His saddlebags lay on the ground, their contents strewn across the sand and sage. He felt his pockets, only to find them turned out and the money he'd kept in one of them gone. His guns were missing too. He stood there a moment, puzzled. It had been the most natural assumption that the man who'd done this was connected somehow to the horse thieves or the Kansas gangs—if they weren't one and the same. But perhaps all it had been was an ordinary robbery.

James set about repacking his saddlebags. He hadn't much in them—a few odds and ends, a spare handkerchief, some matches, and two more sets of the wanted posters.

He'd put everything back inside, except the posters, which were nowhere to be found. He made a small circle around the area, searching, but the papers were gone. He might have surmised they'd blown away, except there was hardly a breeze. It was a perfectly still night. And that left James with only one conclusion to make: the man who'd struck him had stolen not only his money and his guns, but the remainder of the posters.

Ice crawled through his veins. Who would bother to steal such a thing unless his face was on one of them? He'd only been carrying the posters offering rewards for capture of the Fletchers and the Beaumonts, no one else.

Still holding the saddlebags, James peered through the night around him, even though it was clear those responsible were no longer in the vicinity. He was lucky to still be alive. The Fletchers, in particular, weren't known for their mercy.

As he returned the saddlebags to the horse, he supposed it could have been some other sort of outlaw who'd taken the posters in fear of the possibility of his face being among them. But he knew that was wishful thinking. The ambush had been too practiced, too quiet. He hadn't known anyone was upon him until the very last moment. And if that wasn't the work of men who'd been defying the law for upwards of fifteen years, he didn't know what was.

He mounted the horse, nudged him into action, and winced as the movement jarred his aching head. If only he knew which of the Kansas gangs he was dealing with, then he could form some sort of strategy. But one thing did become clear as he rode, and that was where his mind had been right before he was attacked.

Edie.

Was that why he hadn't heard the men coming up from behind him? Not because they were so good at what they did, but because he'd been paying no attention whatsoever to his surroundings? That was a dangerous mistake, and one he knew better than to make. In fact, he'd known better this entire time, and yet that hadn't stopped him. He'd been far too taken with her.

Memories resurfaced as he rode. Ones of Uncle Mark telling James's father about a beautiful woman he'd met and instantly fallen for, and even wanted to marry. His father reassuring Mark he was happy for him and yet questioning how quickly everything was happening. Mark appearing preoccupied at every turn, but with a blissful smile on his face. James's uncle had been county sheriff then, and had been working for a year to finally put an end to the Fletchers' activities in the Flint Hills. James vividly remembered that last night, when Uncle Mark had left the farm to propose to the love of his life, only to find it had all been part of an elaborate trap. Georgia Fletcher had led Mark to his death, ending the life of the one man who'd ever come close to discovering where her brothers and cousins were holed up. And Mark had never suspected a thing.

His sweet Edie was no Georgia Fletcher, but he was acting just as his uncle had. He'd been distracted to the point of obliviousness. He could have easily been killed. And even before tonight, had he been fully present as he walked the town, talked to the people there, kept his ears and eyes open for anything out of the ordinary? Or had his mind been elsewhere, set on a pair of kind brown eyes and fair skin?

He was taking the same path his uncle Mark had. And if he wasn't careful, he'd meet his own end sooner than he wanted.

Chapter Twenty

James came neither to lunch nor dinner in the dining room, and that was when Edie began to worry. Something must have happened to him. What that was, she didn't much care to think on for very long. But there wasn't a way she could simply ask after him to the desk clerk or the stable hands.

She'd created another mixture of peppermint and crushed sagebrush leaves the night before, suspecting he'd used most of what she'd given him earlier. It calmed her mind from thoughts of her family and the news of the horse thieves. And now, it presented the perfect opportunity to ensure he was all right.

If she could find a way around the rules of propriety, that was.

After debating all through the dinner service, Edie finally made up her mind. She'd grown up with a family who saw the law as optional, so it wasn't as if she'd never broken a rule before. Besides, she was hardly breaking an edict that would result in injury to anyone or anything. And this wasn't self-serving; she was truly worried for him. If he wasn't back at the hotel, she needed to alert someone.

But if she was going to bend the rules of propriety just about as far as they could go, she'd need an accomplice. Thinking through her friends as she cleared her last table, she settled on Millie. She was the clear choice, given that she'd bent many a rule herself, and she likely understood Edie's feelings toward James better than Edie herself did. Besides, Millie was always up for an adventure.

And sure enough, Millie readily agreed to Edie's plan.

They waited until an hour after curfew. Beatrice was fast asleep, thankfully, when Edie moved through the darkness of their room, still fully dressed, and slipped out the door. Millie waited near the landing at the top of the stairs, her bright red hair pulled back into a braid for the night and a smile lighting up her face.

"I've only seen one person come upstairs," she said. "But don't worry, I scooted around the corner before he spotted me. The desk clerks rotate at midnight. Mr. Graham will be taking over from Mr. Peterson, so we should have plenty of time before Mr. Peterson comes up."

Edie bit her lip. Only Millie would know the desk clerks' evening schedule.

They walked like wraiths across the landing and stopped to peer around the corner into the south wing, which housed both guests and male employees of the hotel. No one was in sight. With a deep breath, Edie led the way down the hall. James's room, number 210, wasn't very far. Before she knew it, Edie stood, heart pounding so hard she could hear it in her ears, outside his door.

She had a moment of doubt, standing here with her fist poised to knock. It was beyond improper, showing up at a man's door, particularly this late at night. Even if she did have Millie with her, she couldn't possibly explain this away if she were to be caught. And even more, a small part of her feared James might think poorly of her for doing such a thing.

"Knock," Millie whispered.

Edie hesitated again, the tea mixture clutched tightly in her other hand. She finally swallowed and rapped lightly on the door, praying with all her might that first, he was inside, and second, he wouldn't think any less of her for this.

A moment passed, and all fear of impropriety began to slip away as real terror that something must have happened to him took its place. She glanced quickly at Millie, who nodded.

Edie raised her hand to knock again when a click sounded from the door.

Relief washed through her, so hard she braced herself with a hand on the doorframe. The door opened just a crack, and there he was. Here. Alive.

The door opened wider, and he stood in nighttime disarray. She could tell he'd hurriedly dressed, and his hair looked as if he'd been asleep for hours.

"Did I wake you? I'm so sorry to bother you."

"You're no bother." He rubbed a hand across his eyes and gave her a quick smile before letting it fall into a frown. "You shouldn't be here."

That little bit of fear lit inside Edie's heart again. What if he thought her too brazen? "I know this isn't proper, but I worried and I needed to see if you were all right. I didn't come alone." She gestured to Millie, who stood just to her side.

James stepped forward. Millie smiled at him. He nodded politely at her before peering down the hallway.

"You can't stand out here," Millie said, following his gaze. "Go, talk quickly inside, and I'll keep watch out here. I'll knock if someone is coming."

"That's not—" James started, but Millie interrupted.

"It's not proper, I know that. I'm fairly certain Edie does too. But unless you want to rouse every man in this hallway, I suggest you hold your conversation inside your room." She stood, hands on her hips, her gaze bouncing between James and Edie. "Tonight would be nice, as some of us might like to return to our beds."

Edie tried not to smile. Millie was a force unto herself. She'd even stunned James into silence. Finally, he stood back and opened the door wider. Edie stepped quickly inside.

When he shut the door, the room descended into darkness. The floor creaked as he moved across it, and after a brief moment, a lamp flickered to life.

"I'm so sorry," she said again. "I almost didn't come, but you had me fearful that something had happened to you. And besides, I made you more tea." She held up the bag, as if it might explain away her rash actions.

He set the lamp on the night table and reached for the little bag. "I can't thank you enough for this. It's—you've . . . changed my life." He caught her eyes and she thought she might have forgotten how to breathe.

He placed the little bag on the night table next to the lamp.

Edie stood uncertainly near the door. She'd accomplished her purpose in coming here—given him the tea mixture and reassured herself that he was all right. But it wasn't enough. She needed to know more. "I'm glad you're unhurt. Did you find the horse thieves?"

"I didn't. But they may have found me."

She tilted her head. "What do you mean?"

He ran a hand through his hair, mussing it up even more, and suddenly, all Edie could think about was the way it touched his collar and how badly she wanted to fix it for him. She clenched her hands in the folds of her skirt.

"Someone ambushed me after I left the camp."

"Are you . . . you aren't hurt?" Her eyes searched him for signs of injury. "How could that have happened?" He was so alert when they'd ridden from the camp together.

"I've got quite the bump on the head, but that's all." He said nothing more, but something in his face went a bit distant.

Edie fought the urge to close the space between them. It felt so far. *He* felt so far away. Something was different, but she couldn't quite figure out what. "Why would they have done that?" she finally asked.

He shrugged. "I came to only to find they'd taken my guns, some money, and the wanted posters I'd had in the saddlebags."

Edie tried not to show any reaction to that last item. "And you think it was the same men who stole those horses?"

"I've no way to know for certain, but they're likely suspects."

Her throat went dry, and a new question seemed to burn in her throat. "You don't suppose it was . . .?" She trailed off, unable to speak her family name out loud.

"The Fletchers or the Beaumonts? I don't know for certain, but I have my suspicions. I only wish I knew which of them was causing all this trouble. It might make tracking them down a lot easier."

The walls seemed to grow closer, and the room suddenly seemed too warm. Edie lifted a hand to her collar as if that could help her breathe.

"I'm sorry, I didn't mean to scare you." He was there in front of her now, one hand reaching for hers, no longer looking so distant.

"It's . . . it's quite all right," she managed to say, even though it still felt as if there weren't enough air in the room. She felt strangely responsible for what had happened to him. Perhaps if she weren't here, he wouldn't have been hurt. It was a ridiculous notion, some still-functioning part of her brain told her. It might not even be her family at all. And even if it was, it was unlikely they knew she was here.

Unless Mr. Adkins had called her bluff.

Still, if it were her father or one of her brothers or even Nick who'd done this to James, she'd feel terrible. A dangerous desire to tell him everything rose in her mind again, just as it had out in the valley several nights ago. What would he say if he knew? Would he ever look at her again, much less take her hand?

What would happen if this went further? If, after he began to court her in earnest this fall, he proposed marriage? Could she keep this a secret forever?

Could she live with herself if she did?

The words bubbled in the back of her throat. If only she could find the courage to speak them aloud.

Chapter Twenty-one

Edie's jaw worked, as if she wanted to say something. The soft brown eyes behind her spectacles looked over his shoulder, but it was clear her thoughts were far away from here. While any sane-minded person knew to keep their distance from the Fletchers and the Beaumonts, Edie seemed downright terrified each time the subject arose. And this wasn't the first time James had noticed this reaction. It was almost as if she'd had firsthand experience with them. Almost as if she'd lost someone too . . .

"Edie?" James said gently, her hand still in his. It took conscious effort not to envelop her in his arms.

Her eyes flicked back to him, but her face remained serious.

"Have you had a run-in with the Fletchers or the Beaumonts? You look scared to death." He paused as she glanced away again. "I don't mean to dredge up what might be painful memories. You don't have to tell me if it's too much."

"I don't . . ." She shook her head. "I can't . . ." Her sweet face looked up at him again, her eyes filled with unshed tears behind her glasses and her lips pressed stubbornly together.

James let his gaze travel down to their intertwined hands. He so rarely spoke about Uncle Mark that it was hard to find the right words. "I've mentioned my uncle. It's been a few years since he died, but sometimes it feels like yesterday."

She said nothing, but her hand tightened around his. It gave him the courage he needed to press forward. "It was the Fletchers. He was too close to them, too close to finding out where they'd hidden themselves away in the Flint Hills. They lured him into a trap and shot him."

He looked up to find her watching him. Her eyes still shone as if she were on the verge of crying. She raised her free hand and gently touched the side of his face.

"I'm so sorry," she said, her voice cracking just a little on the last word.

More than anything, he wanted to close his eyes and revel in her touch. But that old anger fired again, somewhere deep down inside. The one that had led on him a trail of vengeance years ago, right after Uncle Mark's death. The one he'd thought he'd extinguished, when he'd finally given up revenge to pursue a life serving the law. It reminded him he needed to make a choice.

He'd almost met his fate outside the mining camp last night. If he'd been in his right mind, he might not have found himself knocked out and robbed. And he'd been lucky.

He could've been dead.

James caught Edie's hand and gently lowered it. He stood a moment, soaking in everything she gave him—compassion, sweetness, and, possibly, her heart. He wavered a moment, unwilling to break any of that. It would be so easy, and so *perfect* to wrap her into his arms and hold her close. He shut his eyes, trying to still his mind. Trying to find some semblance of logic that would tell him what he needed to do.

But it was hard to think straight. This was too much. Her, being here. She smelled of roses, although heaven only knew how that could be considering it was barely spring.

"James?" Her lovely voice saying his name sent his mind whirling.

"I need to— You should go." He forced himself to drop both of her hands and take a step back. The rose scent dissipated some, and he gulped air like a man dying of thirst.

"Yes," she said uncertainly.

And all he could think about was how pretty she looked with her hair falling down around her confused face.

"I'll let you know if I hear anything new." His voice was more gruff than he'd intended it to be.

She shrunk toward the door as if his words had hit her in the stomach. A horrible ache rose up inside, and he yearned to take them back, to press his lips to hers and reassure her all was well.

Except it wasn't. He turned abruptly to force the temptation away.

"Good night," she said, her voice tenuous.

He said nothing. He couldn't trust himself when he wasn't sure what would come out of his mouth. His muscles strained with the effort of remaining still until he heard the door click shut.

Only then did he turn around.

His room was empty, save for himself. It was lonely, and he hated it.

But it was the only way.

Chapter Twenty-two

It was still early when Edie slipped out the kitchen door. The sun glittered on the wet blades of grass and bunches of sage. She pulled on a pair of gloves, shivering a bit in the chill, and trying not to think about how strangely James had acted last night.

It was as if something had changed in an instant. One moment, he was holding her hand and speaking softly to her, and the next, he'd turned away and hadn't even bid her good night. The memory cut through her heart, and for the hundredth time since last night, she wondered what she'd done.

But try as she might, she couldn't figure it out.

The little town was quiet as she headed toward it, down the hill to the tracks. Mrs. Ruby wouldn't be happy she'd ventured out alone. She'd hesitated, more because of the promise she'd made herself to remain safely at the hotel than for Mrs. Ruby's rules. But she needed the fresh air and the solitude. And besides, it was too early for anything untoward to happen—and much too early for any of her brothers to be up and about. Provided they were even anywhere nearby. All she wanted to do was go to the mercantile, inquire about ordering seeds for a garden, and then return to the hotel.

Still, she kept her eyes open and her wits about her, just in case.

She couldn't tell James the truth last night. Her heart wouldn't let her, especially after what he'd told her about his uncle. It didn't matter that it hadn't been her family. While the story had shocked her, she was also unsurprised at the violence and deception from the Fletchers. It was how they operated.

If the Fletchers were responsible for the trouble being reported, she thought there would be word by now of more fighting and more indiscriminate shooting. They tended to blaze their way through whatever county they'd landed in, while Edie's family worked more quietly.

The fact that James's ambush was the only real violence that had taken place didn't bode well—not for Edie.

She picked her way over the railroad tracks as the memory of the anguish in James's face resurfaced. She would never forget it, not as long as she lived. He'd said it felt as if it had happened only yesterday, and the emotions he wore on his face made it absolutely clear it was a loss that haunted him. Edie wasn't a Fletcher, but she felt responsible in some way. Her family was so often lumped together with the Fletchers that it became difficult for outsiders to separate them. And knowing she still held her secret from him—a secret that might break him if he knew—intensified the guilt that pervaded her senses each time she thought about his uncle's death.

Had he felt that from her somehow? Maybe that was why he'd backed away so suddenly.

A movement off across the tracks caught her attention and she stilled. But it was only one of the men helping to build the land office. Edie pulled in a deep breath, but walked the rest of the way to the mercantile as if her pa lurked around every corner.

The mercantile door stood open when she arrived. Edie paused outside to check her shoes for mud. Satisfied she wouldn't track any into the store, she took one step inside and stopped still, unable to comprehend what she saw in front of her.

The store had been ransacked. There was no other way to put it. Glass jars were smashed on the floor, shelving had been pushed over, the peppermint candies that normally sat in a bowl on the counter were strewn about and crushed, and various items from shovels to hats to sweet-smelling soaps lay all about.

Edie's breathing quickened and she dug her fingers into her reticule. Panic began to rise inside. She shoved it down. She needed to find out what had happened, and then she could panic if she needed to.

Stepping over broken glass and merchandise, she made her way to the counter where Caroline Drexel stood with bills in her hand, counting them.

Edie waited until Caroline was done before speaking. "What happened here?"

"Oh!" Caroline's head jerked up and a hand went to her heart. "Edie. I'm so sorry, you startled me. I'm afraid I'm a little on edge after . . ." She gestured around her.

"I can see why." Edie's voice shook a little, and she coughed into her elbow in an effort to disguise her nerves.

Caroline tapped the bills into a neat stack. "Early this morning, we awoke to the sound of people downstairs. It wasn't long before we started hearing glass shatter and the shelves being turned over. Thomas went downstairs, but one of them knocked him over the head." She glanced about the room. "I'm grateful he wasn't more hurt, and very happy they didn't venture upstairs."

Edie's palms were damp under her gloves and she could barely swallow. James had also been hit on the head. "Did they . . . What did they take?" She couldn't meet Caroline's eyes as she spoke, instead letting them wander over the mess in the store.

"It's hard to tell, but right now, it seems as if it was only some provisions. They didn't find the bit of money we had behind the counter." Caroline replaced the bills in a wooden box and set it somewhere below where Edie could see. "I only wish they hadn't made such a mess. I don't understand how anyone can find joy in destroying someone else's life's work."

She couldn't imagine what all of this felt like to Caroline. She had to have been terrified last night, and now to see all their hard work crushed and ruined . . . Edie wanted to go behind the counter and give her friend a reassuring hug.

But guilt snaked around her heart and she couldn't do it. Even though she had nothing to do with what had happened here, she could almost see the scene playing out before her. Ty heaving a set of shelving over while Zeb whooped and aimed glass jars at the door. Pa would've been more practical, gathering tinned food and ammunition and new boots. He'd say the boys just needed to let off some steam. Cousin Nick would've been the one who struck Mr. Drexel. He also would've been the one looking for money. If he hadn't found it, he would've gone searching upstairs. Something must have scared them off before he could. He wouldn't have hurt Caroline, but she was still glad her friend was spared that fear.

"It's quite a mess, isn't it?" Caroline said softly, her elbows resting on the counter. "I don't know where to start in putting things back to rights."

That, at least, was something Edie could help with. "My shift doesn't begin until lunch today. Let me find some of the other girls who are free this morning and we can help you."

"Oh, would you? That would be wonderful." Caroline smiled, and Edie's heart lifted some. She couldn't take back what her family had done, but she could at least help clean it up.

"Did you alert Deputy Wright yet?" Edie hesitated in offering to do this for Caroline, especially after how strangely their visit had ended last night. And because she didn't know if she could speak to him about what had happened here without giving away the sense of responsibility she felt for it, as misplaced as it might be.

"That's where Thomas is now. I imagine they'll return soon."

Edie reassured her friend she'd come back with help and made her way back to the door. When she stepped outside, she stood for a moment with her back pressed against the door.

If her family was here in Crest Stone, it could only be for one reason.

Edie narrowed her eyes against the growing morning sunlight as she examined the area around the store. She stepped away from the wall and peered around the corner toward the east, as if Pa or her brothers were hiding just beyond the building. They wouldn't be, not now. Not after the mess they made here. They knew better than that. No, they were likely hidden out somewhere outside of town, biding their time.

For what, she didn't know. Did they only want to speak with her? Or did they have plans to force her to return to Kansas with them?

Or worse, were they hoping to use her knowledge of the hotel as a means to execute some plan to rob the place blind?

Mr. Adkins had clearly given her away. And once her family surfaced again, they'd find her. Everyone would know who she really was, and from what circumstances she'd come. Edie Dutton would be gone forever, along with all the promise of a good, honest life. Her friends would want nothing to do with her. Her employer would regret giving her a second chance. And James . . .

Her heart contracted and she sagged against the side of the mercantile. He'd want nothing to do with her. And after what had happened to his uncle, would he think she was doing the same to him? She squeezed her eyes shut against the tears that threatened. She would never do such a thing, but the evidence would be stacked against her. He'd never believe otherwise.

And perhaps he'd be right.

She wouldn't have done it on purpose, but if her father or brothers caught wind of anything between them, they wouldn't hesitate to make him regret any attention he'd paid her.

James's life. The future of the hotel. The safety of her friends. It was all in danger.

She could leave. Take a horse and ride as far as she could and then board a train to some new place. But if they found her here, they'd find her anywhere. There could always be another Mr. Adkins.

She couldn't escape Edith Beaumont.

And it was time she accepted the only fate she had. She'd give her pa and cousin and brothers what they wanted, and maybe they'd leave without causing any further harm.

She'd give them her future.

Chapter Twenty-three

The Crest Stone Mercantile and General Store was in worse shape than James had imagined. It was hard to find a place to step without crushing something underfoot.

Even more disturbing was Drexel's recounting of what had happened the night before. It was eerily similar to what had happened to James on the ride back from the camp. Unfortunately, neither Drexel nor his wife had gotten a good look at the perpetrators. It was clearly the work of more than one man, but that was all James could piece together.

Frustrated, he left the building to search for any sort of clues the men might have left outside. There would be no tracks, not with the sheer number of men and horses that traversed the road that ran the length of the train tracks. There was nothing else out here that gave even a hint of who the men might be. More than anything, he wanted to form a posse and go after these men. But how could he if he didn't know which family it was or where they'd gone? James clenched his hands. Irritation welled up inside him, threatening to burst.

He ran a fist into the wall, barely wincing at the pain that shot through his knuckles. He had to do something to prevent this from happening again, and he couldn't do that alone.

Rubbing his fingers, he tried to steady his breathing as he looked around the town. *His* town. It didn't matter that he hadn't been here long, and no one here had elected him. He felt some sort of ownership over the peace of this place, and he couldn't abide anyone stealing from its residents or harming them.

That old anger subsided some, and his mind chugged back into clear thought. Signs pointed toward the Beaumonts. Considering both he and Drexel had come out of their run-ins alive and relatively unhurt, and considering the horse thefts—the Beaumonts' usual fallback—it didn't have the signs of the louder, more violent work of the Fletchers.

He couldn't be completely certain, of course, but at least it was a place to start. He'd call a meeting, get some men to stand guard at night. And then he'd telegraph Ben and ask him to send Harry or Eli. He could use the backup.

Spurred on by the plan, he stepped out into the road, only to be met by a group of women. He recognized several of their faces from the hotel. They all wore plain working dresses, and some of them carried rags and buckets and brooms. And there, at the rear of the group, he spotted Edie.

"Good morning, ladies." He tugged the brim of his hat. "Might I ask where you're off to?"

"The general store, Deputy," Miss Barnett answered him. "Miss Dutton said the Drexels needed help cleaning up."

He caught Edie's eye. She gave him a slight, sad smile before turning away. He should've known. Edie had a heart of gold. "Then I wish you well." He nodded at them and watched as they made their way to the store.

Edie lagged behind the group. When she glanced behind her, he took the few steps between them and took hold of her hand. She looked down at his fingers clasped around hers and gently tugged her hand away. "Please don't," she said, so low he could barely hear her.

Her words cut through everything that had made sense only a few minutes ago to a place that was raw and lonesome. He shouldn't have done that, not after the way he'd left things between them last night. He shifted, letting his hand rest on the handle of his revolver, and attempted to look as if he had control of the situation. As if he had control of his heart.

"I think it's the Beaumonts," he said, his voice strained.

She nodded, and a flicker of emotion flashed across her face so quickly he couldn't determine what it meant. "I thought as much too."

There it was again. The indication that there was something in her past, something painful—just like what he carried with his uncle's death. Only hers, it appeared, stemmed from something the Beaumonts had done. "What is it?" he asked.

When she didn't answer, he pressed on. "I've seen it plain as day on your face, more than once. They've done something to you. Or to your family or someone you loved."

She chewed on her lip and cast her eyes down to the hands clasped in front of her.

"I know how it feels. I know what that kind of pain can do." If only she'd tell him, he might be able to help. Even though he knew—*knew*—he needed to keep his distance, he couldn't let her hurt like that without at least trying to help. In fact, it cut him to the core to think that anyone had ever hurt Edie. And if she told him who it was, he'd ensure they'd regret it if he found them.

"I can't say. Please, leave it be." She raised her eyes to meet his.

He was torn between sympathy and irritation. He wanted both to scoop her into his arms and to shake some sense into her all at the same time. "Fine," he said evenly.

"James." Her voice trembled a little on his name. "It was good to meet you. You are more than I ever deserved."

Her words were like a boulder to the gut. He shifted his stance, raising his eyes to look out past the edges of the town where the railroad tracks and telegraph wires disappeared into the distance, acting as if she hadn't crushed any tiny shred of hope he might have remaining. *It was good to meet you.* Something about it sounded so final, as if she thought she'd never see him again. But it was the last sentence she'd spoken that made his heart ache. She was the most wonderful woman he'd ever met, and the thought of her thinking anything less than that of herself was more than he could bear.

Struggling not to convey his emotions with his voice, he finally spoke. "You deserve more than I can give."

She dipped her head, and he couldn't catch her reaction.

He nodded to the girls who waited outside the store for her. "You ought to join your friends."

She turned to look behind her.

"Edie?"

Slowly, she glanced back at him.

"I promise you I'll find them." It would be a hard promise to keep, given how long the Beaumonts had evaded capture in Kansas. But he couldn't let her go with whatever memories she carried haunting her forever. "Stay close to the hotel. Tell the other girls the same."

"I will."

And with that, she left. He watched her join her friends and enter the store, and not once did she look backward. He'd hurt her badly last night. So much so that she sensed his thoughts and put an end to it all for him today.

It was what needed to happen. He knew that, and yet he hated it. But what he'd said was true—she deserved far more than a man whose work came first. A man whose every thought and every movement required complete awareness of his surroundings.

It was better this way. Now he could find the Beaumonts, put an end to their terrorizing, and move forward with his own dream of being elected marshal.

Yet somehow, the moment Edie disappeared into the mercantile, his plans—the ones that had driven him from Kansas to Cañon City, the ones that had dictated the last several years of his life—felt hollow.

But it was all he had now. He adjusted his hat and strode toward the depot. He'd find the Beaumonts even if he drew his last breath in the process. It wouldn't be just for him, it would be for the whole town. For the entire state of Kansas.

For Edie.

Chapter Twenty-four

Edie paused on the edge of town, feeling much the same as she had late last summer when she'd left home. She was on a borrowed horse in the dead of night, praying no one was awake to see her. The only difference now was that she carried food and water instead of money and clothing. And she had no need of a falsified letter of reference.

She gave Crest Stone one last glance before riding out into the night. She ached at the thought of leaving, but she knew this was her only choice. If all her family wanted was her return, they could leave immediately. And if they were hoping to use her to get to the hotel, well . . . she would talk them out of it. If it meant her friends would be safe and James wouldn't need to put himself into danger, she would return home a thousand times.

It wasn't the life she wanted, but it was the life fate had chosen for her.

Edie followed the tracks south of town for a while. She had a short list of places to search, the most likely places her Pa and Nick would've picked to hole up in. The old cabin south of Crest Stone was the easiest place to start, and, it seemed, the most likely choice. Abandoned and off quite a ways from the tracks, it was still an easy ride to Crest Stone. If they weren't there, she'd move up into the mountains. She wouldn't stop looking until she found them and put an end to the fear that now rippled through the town.

It didn't take long to find the cabin, since she knew where it was situated. But as she rode up, she could tell it was empty. No light shone from the windows, no smoke curled from the chimney, and no horses stood in the corral outside the barn.

Edie paused by the barn and considered her options. There were several old fur traders' cabins up in the mountains. They would be much harder to find; it might take her days to locate them. But she had no other choice, so she nudged the horse around the barn and headed toward where the mountains rose like the shadows of giants to the west.

She didn't fear the dark or the wilderness—she'd spent plenty of time in both back in Kansas. What she did fear was the unknown. How would Pa react when she returned? Would he be angry or happy to see her? She tried to focus on what good might come out of this. She'd missed her mother and her brothers so much at times that it seemed her heart might break open. She would get to see them again.

Crest Stone, and everyone in it, would be safe. Her friends could continue to work at the hotel. They'd be able to see the town grow. And James . . .

She almost winced at the ache that tore through her. Instead, she gripped the reins harder and let her eyes shut for just a second. Her actions meant James wouldn't be caught in the middle of this. He'd be alive and unhurt. He could see his plans through, become town marshal, make his uncle's memory proud. She wouldn't have to hurt him with the knowledge that he'd once thought of courting the daughter of one of Kansas's most notorious outlaws. He would be free to find another girl, one who didn't have to lie about her name and her family. He could marry and have a family. He could be happy.

She tried to find the joy in those thoughts, but it was hard to come by. James would forget her in time. In fact, he'd already pulled away from her, she reminded herself. She didn't know why, but now she thought perhaps he'd sensed something not entirely honest about her. And then earlier, when he'd pushed her to confide in him . . . She hadn't, of course, and then he'd grown cold.

He thought that she had been a victim of the Beaumonts, and he'd been upset she refused to tell him. Or perhaps that was only a ruse to get her to own up to something entirely different. He couldn't know she was a Beaumont, but he sensed something was wrong. It was part of his job to know when someone wasn't telling the truth. He'd sensed her lie.

Edie led her horse around a small hill and then past the smattering of pines that sat at its base. She was just beginning to ponder her options for crossing Silver Creek when the shadows in front of her moved.

Every muscle in her body stiffened as fear shot through her like a bullet. She pulled gently on the reins to halt her horse. The animal stamped and huffed as it noticed the figure ahead of it.

It was a man on horseback. A man holding a rifle that pointed straight at her.

"Raise your hands," he said, his voice carrying across the small distance between them. "That horse moves an inch, I'll pull the trigger."

Edie did as he said. But instead of feeling relieved she'd found her family, something felt . . . wrong. She didn't recognize the man's voice.

But that was ridiculous. Her pa and Nick took on men unrelated to the family from time to time to help fill out their numbers. Some jobs needed more bodies. This might be one of them.

She found her voice buried somewhere beneath layers of fear and regret. "I'm Edith Beaumont. I'm here to see my pa."

"Edith Beaumont." The man repeated her name as if he was chewing on the words. He moved closer on horseback, that rifle still raised. "That might be the last name I expected to hear out here."

Edie wrinkled her forehead. Surely the family had let this man in on their plans. Unless . . . Panic curled open like a spring flower deep inside her, expanding until it filled every limb. Her hands began to shake as she held them aloft.

It was impossible. No, not impossible, only improbable. She'd ruled it out this morning. Even James had come to the same conclusion.

"Tell me, Edith Beaumont—" His voice was honey, sliding over the words too sweetly and covering up something far more sinister. "Is your pa around these parts?"

She said nothing. She'd made the wrong decision. A very, *very* wrong decision.

The man stopped now, having drawn even with her horse. He still held that rifle pointed at her, and while his hat covered his eyes, it didn't obscure the dirty blond beard that covered his chin or his cat-who-got-a-mouse grin. "'Cause I owe him a little something for that bullet he put in my leg a couple years back."

And with that bit of information, Edie knew who she'd stumbled across for certain.

Levi Fletcher.

Chapter Twenty-five

James fumbled for the pocket watch on the night table. 3:44 a.m. Trying to sleep was pointless. Each time he drifted off, he woke again, besieged with doubts.

He pushed aside the bedclothes and stood. He thought he'd at least feel at peace with his decision, but peace seemed something far out of his grasp. He rubbed his face and moved to the window. It was dark as sin outside, and even though he knew the stables lay not too far away and the mountains rose off to the right, just barely within sight of his window, he could see none of it.

He raised his hands to grip the window frame and let the worries tumble through his mind. Had he done the right thing, letting Edie go as he did? It had seemed right in the light of day, but now . . .

She had made the decision, though, not him. It wouldn't have been right to press her, not when she'd had her mind made up. But perhaps she'd only put distance between them after he'd been so cold with her the night before.

James turned and faced the door to his room. She'd stood right there, some thirty hours ago or so. She'd cast aside all fears of impropriety or a ruined reputation to ensure he wasn't hurt and to bring him the herbs he needed to do his work. And his response had been to push her away. Of course she'd put an end to all of it yesterday. What else could she have done after he'd acted the way he did?

But it was for the best, wasn't it? It was what he'd wanted—to clear his mind so he could focus on the job he needed to do. Yet somehow that focus still eluded him, because now all he could think of was what he'd lost. Edie's sweet smile. The times he'd made her laugh. Her passion for plants and for books. The easy way they'd conversed for hours on the road to Cañon City. How quick she'd been to follow his lead when they'd ridden out from the mining camp. Her bravery in even going to such a place. The way she had little regard for so-

106

cietal conventions when they didn't suit her. How she seemed to always think of others first, including him. The sweet feel of her hand in his, as if she trusted him to protect her from everything bad in this world.

He turned back to the window and pressed his forehead to the glass. It was cool and just what he needed. He closed his eyes and let the feeling calm the tumult in his head.

He'd been operating on the fear that Edie would keep him distracted from his work. But was it her, or was it the not knowing? Not knowing how to carve out a career while caring so deeply about someone, not knowing what the future might bring, not knowing what a life together might look like. He'd been torn between knowing that while Sheriff Young seemed to accomplish his duties as county sheriff just fine with a wife by his side, his uncle hadn't been able to do any such thing.

But that wasn't real.

James straightened at the revelation. The love Uncle Mark felt for Georgia Fletcher was real, but it hadn't been returned. It had been a setup. He'd been led into complete infatuation with that woman—on purpose. That wasn't what James had with Edie at all. Perhaps he'd been looking at the entire situation wrong. Perhaps what he and Edie had was more akin to Ben and his wife.

Maybe it was possible to have both love and his work.

He needed to speak with her. To apologize for the way he'd acted. And to confess his true feelings for her. She could still turn him down, but at least then he'd know he'd given it everything he could. And maybe—just maybe—she'd accept him. With time, she'd tell him about the pain she was carrying, whatever it was she couldn't seem to put words to yesterday.

A smile lifted his lips as the thought of a life together with Edie flitted through his mind. They could have a house, like the one Hartley was building now, with a little garden out back for Edie to grow her plants. He'd craft bookshelves and help her fill them. Maybe one day there would even be children.

James laughed to himself. He was getting far too ahead. He had to speak with her first, and find out if she felt the same way. She had at one time, of that much he was certain. But whether she still cared for him, that he didn't know.

The minutes ticked by slowly. At six, he finally left the room, having been fully dressed for an hour.

Downstairs, the lobby was empty save for a few hotel employees making their way to the kitchen. Edie did not appear. Time crawled until an hour had passed. She might not be working the breakfast service, but still, she should've come downstairs to eat. Unless she was so angry with him she didn't want to leave her room. He needed to find out.

James strode across the lobby toward the hallway where he'd seen the employees heading for the last hour. He'd just turned into it when a door, ahead on the left, flew open. McFarland, Mrs. Ruby, and a young, petite waitress emerged, deep in conversation.

"Deputy!" McFarland said the moment he spotted James in the hallway. "We were just coming to find you."

Taking in the women's worried looks, James knew it wasn't anything good. "How can I help?"

"One of our girls is missing," McFarland said in his Irish brogue. Nearly always in a suit with his hair neatly combed, this morning was no different. The man looked ready to sit down and dine with the president.

Before James could speak, the younger woman piped up. "She's my roommate. She was there last night, but when I awoke this morning, she was gone. I thought maybe she'd come downstairs early, but she isn't here."

"We've sent people out to check the stables, the springhouse, and even through the town," the older woman added.

"One of the horses is missing," McFarland said. "Mrs. Ruby said the girl isn't given to wander, although she's been in a spot of trouble here before."

"What sort of trouble?" From what Edie had told him, James knew there were about a hundred ways the girls could break the stringent rules set by the hotel. Everything from wearing a dirty apron at a meal service to one he knew all too well, meeting with a man in secret.

Mrs. Ruby looked to McFarland. The man gripped the edges of his jacket and lowered his voice. "There was an incident late last year in which the girl had been made to steal from the hotel by one of our former stable hands."

James fought to keep his expression neutral. That was about the last thing he'd expected to hear. Given the tight ship McFarland ran here, he had a hard time imagining such a person remaining employed at the hotel. "And yet she's still here?"

McFarland's face grew stony. "I believe in second chances, Deputy. And this girl had been put in a terrible position against her will. The only thing she did wrong was to not come to me or Mrs. Ruby right away."

"She felt she had no other option," Mrs. Ruby said gently. "The man told her that her family owed him money. I believe he threatened to damage her reputation if she spoke out. And she's an excellent waitress."

"She's a good person," the younger girl added. She had a strange expression about her as she looked at James, one he couldn't place at all. "A good friend, and she works hard here. I'm worried sick about her. It isn't like her to just disappear."

James nodded. Far be it from him to pass judgment on a woman he didn't know. "I'll round up a couple of men to help with the search. Do you have any idea in what direction she might have gone?"

"Not in the slightest," Mrs. Ruby said.

"We asked around. No one seems to know where she might have gone," McFarland added.

James stifled the urge to groan. It would be like searching out a single blade of grass in an entire field. But he'd start with the most obvious directions—the roads to Cañon City and the mining camp. "May I have the girl's name?"

"Edie Dutton," Mrs. Ruby replied.

The air seemed to leave the room. James stared at the woman until she wrinkled her forehead in confusion.

"Deputy, are you quite all right?" she asked.

His eyes moved across the group, searching for any hint that Mrs. Ruby had spoken the wrong name. McFarland looked ready to step forward and offer assistance. And the girl merely looked at him with a sympathetic expression. That was why she'd looked so strangely at him before. She was Edie's roommate, and most likely her confidant.

He needed to pull himself together. He straightened and forced himself to nod. "Quite fine, thank you, ma'am. I'll put together a team of men and begin searching. McFarland, could I borrow some of your off-duty employees?"

McFarland readily agreed. The group dispersed and James returned to the lobby. It wasn't until he'd returned to his room to retrieve his coat, the new guns Ben had sent down on a train from Cañon City, and his saddlebags that he let himself think again.

Edie was missing, ridden off to parts unknown. Not only that, but she'd apparently been blackmailed into stealing from the hotel several months ago. That new information boggled his mind. Why hadn't she said anything? From what she'd told him, she wasn't on speaking terms with her family. And then this man showed up and insisted she repay him money her family owed him. And that night in the mining camp . . . she'd been looking for her brothers.

Something about all of this didn't quite add up. But James couldn't expend thoughts on that at the moment, not when he needed to focus on finding her.

Because right now, Edie could be out riding into country where the Beaumonts might be lurking.

He needed to find her before they did.

Chapter Twenty-six

It was just past dawn when they arrived. Edie's arms ached from remaining in the same position for the better part of two hours. Levi Fletcher had bound her hands to the saddle horn and taken her reins to lead her horse behind his.

She'd spent most of the ride angry with herself for making such a foolish decision. They'd been wrong—both she and James—in suspecting it was her family behind all the trouble. It had been the Fletchers, operating in a much quieter manner than usual. And now she'd pay for her hasty choice.

As they'd grown closer, the anger dissolved into fear. What exactly did the Fletchers want with her? Did they plan to take her back to Kansas and ransom her to her family? Would Levi Fletcher use her to draw out her pa and exact his own revenge? Or—she trembled at the thought—would they simply kill her as some sort of horrible message to her family?

When they rounded a copse of aspens and several large boulders, she was imagining her friends having breakfast in the kitchen and preparing for the first meal service of the day. Had she been missed yet? She was scheduled to work the breakfast shift. Surely Beatrice had spoken to Mrs. Ruby by now. She wondered what they would do. Would they wait for her to return? Or would they notify James?

James. What would he think?

The sadness that clawed at her heart disappeared in an instant when they cleared the aspens and rode up to a handful of other men sitting around a fire in front of . . . was that a cave?

But she didn't have time to ascertain what it was, because Levi had already dismounted and was standing by her horse, untying the rope that held her hands to the saddle. He stepped back and stood, waiting, as the other men rose, one-by-one.

"Get yourself down, girl, lest you want me to help you." He leered at her, and that was all Edie needed. She scrambled off the horse, landing off-balance with her hands still tied together, and falling against the animal before righting herself.

"Well, I'll be. That fool rustler was right after all," one of the men said.

"What you bring back a girl for, Levi?" The kid who spoke was no more than a boy. He looked about the same age as Edie's youngest brother, maybe fourteen or so.

"That ain't just a girl." An older man, his dark hair shot through with streaks of silver and his face weathered from years in the Kansas sun, stepped forward. "You're Jonas Beaumont's girl."

It wasn't a question, but Edie nodded slowly. It was futile to deny it, not when the man who'd caught her already knew.

"I remember you," the older man continued, drawing even with Levi. "It was, I don't know, maybe seven years ago. You Beaumonts moved in too close to the Hills, and your pa and I met for a little talk out at his place. You was running around with your ma, a pretty little thing even with those spectacles. Made me wish I had a daughter of my own."

Edie swallowed. She remembered. They'd moved again, this time farther east than they'd ever gone before. But it hadn't been for long. Her pa had that parlay with Virgil Fletcher, the old man standing in front of her now, and then her family had packed up and left, gone back to the western plains.

"You remember," the man said, his face crinkling into a smile.

She'd never felt so many eyes on her at once, except for those horrible moments back in the hotel stables last December when her crimes were discovered. She wanted to disappear now, the same as she did then.

"What's she doing here?" one of the younger men asked. His otherwise handsome face was marred with a scar that stretched from his ear to his mouth.

Virgil Fletcher still smiled at her as he answered. "Why, Tell, she's done run away from home. That's how Adkins put it, anyhow."

Adkins. Edie's heart nearly stopped at the mention of that name. But how could they know . . . "He wrote you," she said, as the realization blossomed. He'd kept his promise and not breathed a word of her whereabouts to her family or the hotel, but he'd told the Fletchers.

"Seems he thought I might take an interest. He worked with us a time or two back in Kansas, after he worked for your pa, and I suppose he felt some sort of loyalty." Virgil Fletcher scratched at his beard, but kept his eyes on her. "Don't much care what his reasons were, but it sure was good information to have."

"Pa, you mean we rode all the way out here for her?" Tell Fletcher looked awfully displeased. "I thought you said we was after something big."

Edie wouldn't have wanted to be in Tell's shoes with the glare Virgil shot him. "Boy, use your head. Jonas Beaumont would kill to get his girl back, all safe and sound. We can do that for him—" His gaze swung back to Edie, and he smiled a bit. "Provided the price is right."

Tell suddenly looked much more interested in her, as did his brothers. It was enough to make Edie want to shrink back into her horse, but she refused to give them the satisfaction of knowing they'd intimidated her. As much as she'd wished to belong to another family her entire life, she was still Jonas Beaumont's daughter. And her pa didn't shrink from anyone, ever. Neither did her mama. So Edie straightened her shoulders and leveled her eyes at Levi. "What's your price?"

He smiled at her in earnest now. "Well, now, look who wants to play." But instead of answering her, he spoke to his son. "Tell, go rouse Jack. If he ain't still drunk from last night, tell him he's going to send a message to Beaumont."

But Edie didn't give in that easily. She rubbed her hands together until the rope began to chafe her wrists. "What are you asking my pa for?"

"That's business between me and your pa, girl."

"I might be able to help."

He narrowed his eyes at her. "You turned your back on your own family. How would you know what they want or don't want these days?"

His words couldn't have hurt more if they'd been a knife slicing into her skin. He was right. She'd done exactly that. And it was a decision she'd wrestled with for months before she actually made it. She loved her family, but she couldn't spend the rest of her life on the run. She wanted no more part in their crimes. All she yearned for was a simple, honest existence somewhere she wouldn't need to look over her shoulder every few minutes.

And she'd had that, at least for a while. It was everything she'd hoped for. Even now, if she was forced to return to Kansas, she'd have the memories of a real life, one with friends, meaningful work, and a man she never could have imagined knowing.

Her heart felt squeezed as she thought of James. Was he looking for her right now? Surely someone at the hotel had told him about Mr. Adkins and her transgressions last year. What did he think of her now?

Tell returned with another man staggering behind him. Whiskey Jack, Edie remembered hearing his name before. He was Virgil's brother, or maybe his brother-in-law, if she remembered correctly. She wondered which of these men had been the one who shot James's uncle.

"Why do I got to be the one to get a message to the Beaumonts?" he said, his voice raspy with sleep.

"'Cause I ain't sending one of the boys," Virgil replied.

"And he knows I'm like to shoot Jonas myself rather than relay a message," Levi added before spitting on the ground.

Virgil rubbed a hand across his face. "Don't take the message to him directly. Last thing we need is them thinking you're an even exchange for the girl. Find some kid in town and pay him."

Whiskey Jack mumbled some sort of agreement, and, with the surly look still on his face, went to saddle one of the horses. Edie watched him as she replayed the conversation in her head. *Pay some kid in town. Like to shoot Jonas myself.* They made it sound as if her pa wasn't in Kansas. Her eyes widened. "My pa's somewhere nearby?"

Levi frowned at her. "Who you think's been making all the trouble? Ain't been us."

"We haven't had no fun at all lately," Tell said from behind Levi.

It *was* her family. So she and James had been right after all—they'd just missed the fact that the Fletchers had, for the first time in their lives, been quiet.

"Seems they got curious about why we crossed the state line and followed us. It's fine by me. Easier than having to take you all the way back to Kansas with us." Virgil turned back to the boys ringed behind him and Levi. "Tell, you're in charge of her. Treat her good. I swear if I hear of any of you boys acting untoward to her, I'll flay you myself."

Tell nodded and the group began to disperse. Levi brushed past Edie and she unconsciously shrunk away from him. He gave her an unpleasant grin and moved closer. She forced herself to remain where she was. She would not give this man the satisfaction of thinking he cowed her. He reached around her for the horse's reins, taking far longer than needed, and every terrible thing she'd ever heard about the Fletchers rose unbidden in her mind.

As Tell reached for her arm to pull her toward the fire, she wondered again which one of them had killed James's uncle. And now here she was, letting Tell Fletcher help her sit awkwardly on the ground and accepting a cup of hot coffee from one of his brothers. Which of these boys had already committed murder? Was the one with the kind smile sitting across from her capable of such a thing? Edie shivered, even with the tin cup of coffee between her still bound hands.

"You cold, Miss Edith?" Tell asked.

She shook her head but he placed a saddle blanket around her shoulders anyway. He was acting kindly toward her now, likely because his pa had told him to. But what would happen if they didn't get what they wanted? What if the message never reached Pa? Or worse, what if it did and he decided she was worthless to him?

She squeezed her eyes shut at the thought. It was possible, after all. She'd run off without a word. He'd be well within his rights to disown her entirely.

Or perhaps Virgil Fletcher would ask for too much, more than Pa could give. What would they do with her then?

She couldn't swallow the coffee. A lump the size of the cave behind her seemed to have lodged in her throat. She clutched the cup between her hands, holding on to it for dear life.

She dared not to hope James might find her. If he was looking, that was. He had to be, though. Despite his feelings toward her, he was duty-bound to search for her if the McFarlands reported her missing.

Edie watched as Levi mounted his horse and left, likely returning to his hiding place down the mountain. Riding to where he'd be sure to see James if the deputy happened to come this way. He wouldn't be so kind to James, though. It would be like walking into a trap.

Same as his uncle.

Edie squeezed the cup in her hand. It wasn't the same, was it? She hadn't led him here on purpose. And she . . . she loved him. Tears pushed at the backs of her eyes as she let the truth of the thought flood through her. If she could, she'd warn him away. Tell him to let this work out as it might. Tell him the truth about herself. Keep him safe, even if it meant he despised her.

But she couldn't. She was stuck on this hard bit of ground, her hands tied, with a passel of Fletchers keeping their eyes on her every move.

There was no getting out of being Edith Beaumont. Not anymore. And now she'd pulled James into it.

He might be killed, and it would be all her fault.

Chapter Twenty-seven

It didn't take long for James to find and prepare enough men to search for Edie, although each minute that ticked by felt like precious time lost forever. He split the group into two, sending one group north toward Cañon City while leading the second group himself eastward, toward the mining camp. As long as he focused on the search and on giving the men he rode with enough information to make them useful, he could hold off the sick, worried feeling that lurked inside him.

But the moment everything went quiet, it returned with a vengeance.

Edie was missing. He didn't know why. And she'd kept a good bit of her recent history from him. That couldn't be why she'd run off. It didn't make sense, considering McFarland told him the man who'd blackmailed her was now in prison and all of it had happened months ago. Had she run off because of James? Because of the way he'd acted toward her?

He'd just seen her yesterday morning, and she hadn't been distraught. Although, he had to admit, she had acted strangely, especially in the way she'd told him it had been nice to meet him. He'd thought it was just an awkward way of informing him he needed to keep his distance, but maybe she knew then that she'd be leaving.

Perhaps she'd already been planning to ride out.

But why? And to what destination?

He shook his head. They had to find her. He could ask her then, demand the entire story from her. But now, he needed to ensure she didn't run into the Beaumonts first.

When they reached the mining camp, he sent one man to inform Marshal Tate of the goings on and dispatched the rest of the group to search the camp. He went directly to the livery, where he'd seen her last. Images of her slight frame wearing men's clothes that were much too big for her flitted through his mind. She'd been so determined to find her brothers. It was a foolish thing to do, yet brave at the same time. He tried to piece that bravery together with the woman who'd stolen from the hotel. It made no sense, and he huffed in frustration.

Mr. Ayers was nowhere to be seen, so he took it upon himself to comb the entire building, inside and out. He rounded the rear of the stables, facing a line of pine trees and beyond that, the rise of the Wet Mountains—and came face-to-face with a man holding a shotgun.

James bit back words of irritation and raised his hands. He had no time for petty thieves, not now. "What do you want?"

The man was tall and lean, and somewhere around James's age. A hat covered dull sand-colored hair, and his green eyes flicked down to the guns sitting on James's hips. He repositioned the shotgun, holding it perfectly level. James doubted much got by this man.

"You the sheriff's deputy? The one from Crest Stone?" the man asked.

"I am," James said slowly. "You looking for me?"

"Might be."

"You care to lower that shotgun, then? I'm more inclined to talk when I'm not being held at gunpoint." James kept his eyes open for any change in the man's movements, anything that might betray whether he'd change his mind and shoot.

"Can't do that, sir. But I need your help."

This was a first. "Care to at least tell me who I'm speaking with?"

"You can call me Tyrone."

No last name, although there was something familiar about the first name. It scratched at the edge of his mind, just out of reach. "All right, Tyrone. I'm listening."

"I hear you're looking for a girl."

James raised his eyebrows. "Do you know her whereabouts?"

"If I did, I wouldn't be asking for your help." The man's words were clipped. "I'd be going to get her myself."

"You know her?" Edie had come here looking for her brothers. Perhaps this was one of them. Tyrone . . . That was where he'd heard the name before. But why the shotgun?

The man ignored James's question. "I know who all's got her. We just don't know where."

A rush of something hot rose inside James. He was too late. "And who would that be?" he asked, trying to keep his voice even.

"Virgil Fletcher and his boys."

James bit back the words he wanted to unleash. It wasn't the Beaumonts after all. He'd been wrong. It was the Fletchers. The thought of her being held against her will by those men made him want to run his fist into the wall—again. If any of them hurt her, so help them, he wouldn't rest until he found each one of them and made him pay.

"I can tell you're thinking the same thing I am," the man said.

"What's your concern with her?" James asked, suspecting he already knew.

"She's my sister."

He'd guessed correctly. "Miss Dutton came looking for her brothers a few days back."

"Miss Dutton?" The man screwed up his face in confusion. "I'm looking for Edith Beaumont."

"Edith . . . Edie . . ." James didn't finish the name. It was as if all the wind had been knocked out of him.

It couldn't be. It was impossible.

And yet, at the same time, it made so much sense.

Chapter Twenty-eight

" It's time." Virgil Fletcher kicked at the backside of the boy sitting nearest the cave. Edie hadn't caught the boy's name, but he was a fidgety one, given to stand suddenly at the most unexpected moments.

Before Edie could ask what was happening, Whiskey Jack brought her horse around. He'd returned an hour ago, right after which he and Virgil had disappeared inside the cave.

Tell reached down for her arm, propelling her to her feet and then asking if she was all right. The boy had been nothing but kind to her, to the point that Edie began questioning all she'd heard about the Fletchers. But then a couple of the boys had recounted some of their exploits back in Kansas as they took turns slinging a knife at a nearby aspen, and Edie was reminded of who exactly she was dealing with.

She'd sat quietly all afternoon on the hard ground, her legs and arms slowly growing numb, and her mind racing through possibilities. What would happen if her pa didn't agree to the Fletchers' terms? What if James attempted to intervene? And the worst one of all—what if the entire premise of a ransom was only an excuse for the Fletchers to exact some sort of revenge on her family? Levi was certainly angry enough. Virgil and the others might feel the same, even if they weren't so vocal about it. And if James were there too . . . The awful images rolled across her mind, unbidden and impossible to stop.

And the longer she sat, the more the worry grew.

"Are you sure you're all right? Tell asked her again.

Edie nodded. Physically, she was fine. In fact, it felt good to stand now, even if her hands were still bound and she had to rely on Tell Fletcher to ensure she remained upright. It was her mind that couldn't settle.

"Where are you taking me?" she asked the boy.

"We got a meetup with the Beaumonts." He led her to the horse, but Edie stopped still and he almost tripped.

She yanked herself around, back toward where Virgil stood with Whiskey Jack and another man she hadn't yet caught the name of. She had to know what they had planned. She refused to go into this unprepared. "Mr. Fletcher," she called, taking a few steps forward before Tell recovered enough to halt her progress.

The men stopped talking.

"Miss Edith, you need to get on the horse," Tell said in a frantic, low voice.

Edie ignored him. "Mr. Fletcher, I demand to know your plans."

That easy grin slid across Virgil's face again as he ambled toward her, the other men following behind.

Edie straightened, Tell's hand still wrapped around her arm. He pulled on her, but she stood firm. "If you're using me as some sort of bait, it's only fair I know what you're planning."

"I already told you, Miss Beaumont. You don't take me at my word?" He crooked an eyebrow.

Edie no more took this man at his word than she'd have taken a snake at his. She said nothing, but she held her head high and refused to look away.

"She don't trust you one bit," Whiskey Jack said with a laugh.

The other man merely stared at her before a slight smile curved his lips.

Edie glanced up at Tell. He wouldn't meet her eyes.

There was nothing trustworthy about these men. For all she knew, they *were* telling the truth. But she couldn't take that chance. She needed to keep them away from her family. Away from James.

"I have a proposal for you," she blurted out.

"A proposal," Virgil repeated, as if he didn't quite comprehend what she'd said.

"Yes. I assume you came here for money, right?"

Virgil didn't reply, but he didn't indicate he was uninterested in what she had to say.

Edie pushed on, making it up as she went. "I work at the hotel as a waitress. I don't know if Mr. Adkins mentioned it in his letter, but I have regular access to the hotel's office. To the safe."

"And what does that mean to us?" the unnamed man asked.

Edie swallowed, hardly able to believe what she was going to say. "It means I can get you money." When none of them responded, she added, "Regularly." Of course, she had no intention of doing anything of the sort, but if the lure of such an idea kept them from this meeting with her family, she'd promise them anything.

"We're set for money, girl. We don't need the pennies you'd collect from the hotel. Besides, ain't one of us got any intention of remaining in these parts." Virgil tapped his fingers against his gun belt and glanced at Tell. He was impatient with the conversation, that much was clear.

As if on cue, Tell tugged at her arm again. But Edie remained planted where she was. She wouldn't give up that easily.

"Then I'll go with you, back to Kansas. I can be useful to you. I could . . . collect information." Her mind spun, trying desperately to come up with something Virgil might latch on to.

"You'd be a spy?" The older man took a few steps forward until he was so close, she could see the individual strands of salt and pepper in his beard. He looked down at her, and she fought the urge to back up. She couldn't cower from him, not if she wanted him to believe her. And so she stood firm, fighting every instinct that told her to do otherwise. "And who would you spy on?"

"Anyone you might need to know more about." Her palms grew damp and her heart thumped a rhythm she thought for certain they could all hear.

"Anyone?" His smile grew broader as if she amused him. "Your own family?"

Edie swallowed. "If needed." She wasn't certain how she'd get out of such a situation, but she'd figure that out later—if this worked.

The smile disappeared. "I got no need for a blood traitor. Besides, I know you ain't got the stomach for it, or you never would've left Kansas." He held her gaze a moment longer, his steely gray eyes so cold that they hardly seemed to belong to anyone living. "Tell," he said without moving. "Get her up on that horse before I lose my temper."

"Yes, Pa." Tell pulled on her arm again, and Edie relented.

She'd failed.

And now both James and her family might pay the price.

Chapter Twenty-nine

Ty Beaumont led James and the other men out of the mining camp. James dispatched a couple of the men to return to Crest Stone to gather more. If they were going to meet up with the Fletchers, he wanted to ensure he had the larger numbers on his side.

At first, he'd wondered if he could trust this Beaumont. But considering Ty let a number of men who might rather see him hanging from the end of a noose ride with him out into the valley—and considering he'd finally put up that shotgun—James was inclined to give him the benefit of the doubt. It had crossed his mind they might be riding into an ambush, but at least he knew Ty wasn't lying about his identity. James had pressed him for details about his sister, and everything he'd said rang true about the woman James knew.

Edie. Or did she prefer Edith? James couldn't even decide if he was angry with her or not. He was far too concerned with her well-being right now to let any other emotion take over, but he couldn't deny the disappointment he felt at her untruthfulness. On the one hand, it made sense. She'd wanted a new life—that much was obvious—and so she'd come here under an assumed name. She likely hardly thought she'd make the acquaintance of a lawman. And it certainly explained her initial reaction to him. He smiled at the memory of her mud-covered self running for the railroad tracks. She probably thought she was protecting her family, and her own reputation, by not telling him the truth.

But as she'd gotten to know him, why had she continued the farce? Didn't she trust him? She hadn't even told him about her troubles at the hotel last fall.

Another thought rose unbidden as his horse plodded along after Ty Beaumont's—would James have trusted her after such a revelation?

He wanted to think he would have, without hesitation. But would he, though, after what had happened to Uncle Mark? He could almost imagine himself reeling away from her, trying to make sense of it. He could hardly comprehend it when Ty had said her name.

James shook his head to clear his thoughts. He'd have time to figure those out later, provided he was successful in this mission. Right now, all that mattered was rescuing Edie from the Fletchers and preventing any bloodshed between the two families. He'd had to promise Ty he'd let the Beaumonts leave unscathed to return to Kansas after this. That would've been harder to agree to if they'd been the ones to put Uncle Mark six feet under. But deep in his heart, James knew he would've done it even then if it meant Edie's safety. He'd do anything for that woman, Beaumont or not. He'd lost himself some time ago, even though it now seemed she'd been bent on breaking his heart.

Well, at least he was being honest with himself.

Ty halted his horse. James drew up even with him and waited as the other man scanned the land ahead.

"They'll be up that way. They likely already saw us. You understand I'd prefer just you and I ride in? I don't think Pa would take too kindly to me bringing up a whole posse."

James considered it. It was a dangerous prospect, agreeing to ride in alone to a den of thieves. But he had his guns. And he was the one who'd have enough men to aid the Beaumonts in rescuing Edie. If they killed him, they'd have no help.

Unless it was a trap.

Despite the way she'd kept so much from him, he refused to believe Edie would set him up in such a way, but he wouldn't put it past these men to steal her away and pin the blame on the Fletchers, just to get him out here, alone. In fact, it sounded right in line with how the Beaumonts operated. "How do I know I'll ride back out of there alive?"

Ty took off his hat and ran a hand through his hair. "Fair enough. You go in alone. I'll stay here with your men."

James nodded. After further instructions, he rode south, into an abandoned mining operation that abutted the mountains—and about six men pointing all manner of firearms at him. James lifted his hands, praying he'd made the right decision.

"Thought you said Ty was with him?" An older, clean-shaven man spoke. Jonas Beaumont, if the pictures were correct.

"He was," a kid of about eighteen or twenty replied. "I saw him with this fella, and a whole bunch of folks from the town."

"He's with my men," James said, looking Jonas Beaumont straight in the eye.

The old man held his gaze. "You're a smart one. Good." He lowered the revolver he held, but didn't return it to its holster. The other men followed suit, and James breathed a little easier as he dismounted.

"Jonas Beaumont," the man said by way of introduction.

"James Wright, Fremont County sheriff's deputy," James said, eying the one younger man who hadn't entirely lowered his shotgun.

Jonas's gaze followed James's. "Zeb," he said tersely, and the man let the gun sink to his side. He turned back to James. "Ty tell you why you're here?"

"He did."

Jonas took a few steps forward, another man with a hat pulled down over his eyes staying close behind. "I want you to know we appreciate your assistance. As soon as I've got my girl back safe, we'll be out of your territory for good."

His girl back. James swallowed as he pictured Edie, headed back to Kansas with these men—her family. Would she want to? He would've thought that was the last thing she wanted . . . until she left the hotel in the dead of night. Considering no one had forced her to leave, he could only assume she'd gone in search of the Beaumonts and found the Fletchers instead.

"I'll take your word on that, provided you leave quietly."

Jonas scratched at his chin and grinned at the man next to him. "All right. My sincerest apologies for that store in town. I sent the boys in for some provisions, and I hear they got a little wild. You know how boys are."

James didn't return the man's smile. His boys had cost the Drexels a lot of money and time, not to mention frightened Mrs. Drexel half to death. "Ty said you were due to meet with the Fletchers."

Jonas's smile disappeared immediately. "That's right. Eight o'clock, at an old homestead south of town."

"Did they say what they wanted?"

Jonas shook his head.

"Likely half our territory," the other man muttered. He pushed back his hat, revealing bright blue eyes in a face that was beginning to show lines. Nick Ford, James recalled. The troublemaker of the bunch.

The last thing James wanted was to get embroiled in the politics of these families, but it seemed inevitable. "Is that something you're willing to cede?"

Jonas shifted uncomfortably while Ford glared at James as if he was the one requesting that payment.

These people turned James's stomach. "I see—"

"No," Jonas said. "But that's only because there won't be negotiations with the Fletchers. That's why you're here."

James furrowed his brow, trying to make sense of the man's words.

"There won't be need for negotiations if we take them by surprise," Jonas explained. "They took my girl. I'm long past mercy."

He should've known. "No," he said, a bit more forcefully than he intended. "If I'm to help you—if I'm to involve all those men waiting back there—we're doing our best to avoid bloodshed. I'm not requiring you to accede to their demands, but only to ride in and at least find out what those are. Do you understand?"

Jonas glanced at Ford, who shook his head.

"They got our sister, Pa," one of the younger men—Zeb, James thought—said.

"You either do it my way or you'll get no help from me," James said. It was a calculated risk. He was going after Edie either way, but the Beaumonts didn't know that.

Jonas kept his eyes on James, as if measuring him up, Finally, he spoke. "We need the numbers. So you've got yourself a deal."

James let out a rush of air. "All right. Let's head out, then. We'll talk strategy on the way."

As the Beaumonts gathered horses and guns, James sorted through options for the millionth time. He didn't know entirely what they were walking into, and this could go so many ways.

His only goal was to get Edie and his men out of there alive.

Chapter Thirty

Edie's eyes strained to see through the shadows dusk had begun to create. One of Virgil Fletcher's boys had called out that the Beaumonts were on their way, but so far, Edie could see nothing.

They were coming for her. She wasn't sure how she felt about that. Pa couldn't have entirely cut her from the family if he was coming to meet with the Fletchers to get her back. While that warmed her heart, she didn't want them here. Even though she'd removed herself from that life when she came to the Colorado Territory, she still loved her family, and she couldn't abide the thought of them potentially setting themselves up for any sort of bloodshed.

Turn around, she prayed, even if, selfishly, she had visions of Pa or Nick plucking her from this horse and riding her off to safety.

Finally, the vaguest outlines of horses, and the dust they stirred up, appeared in the distance. The Fletchers had chosen the abandoned cabin Edie had visited during her search for this meeting, and now she leaned forward from where she stood against the front wall for a better look. A large hand clamped down on her shoulder, pressing her back into place. Levi Fletcher grinned down at her.

"We ain't had our negotiations yet," he said, keeping his hand wrapped around her shoulder.

Edie lifted her shoulders, trying to shake him off, but he held firm. To distract herself from the discomfort, she squinted to try to see the horses and men better.

It only took a few minutes before it became clear how *many* men were riding in this direction. The Fletchers had nine men—Edie had counted each one back up on the mountain. But it looked as if her own family had multiplied in size. She couldn't even imagine who else they'd found to ride in with them.

Virgil Fletcher whistled once, and just like dogs responding to their master, each man drew his weapon.

"No!" Edie shouted, only to have Levi push her back into the wall.

Virgil shot them a stony look. "Hold her."

And before Edie could protest, Levi wrapped his arm around her neck. She sputtered in protest and clawed at it, but it did no good. Her fingers slid uselessly across his coat sleeve and he didn't budge even a fraction of an inch.

The men on horseback rode closer, and as soon as they'd crested the barn, Virgil shouted, "Halt there!" He didn't give away the slightest bit of fear or confusion at the presence of such a large group.

The men came to a stop, and Edie scanned the lot of them, trying to make out faces at such a distance. There was Pa, tall and sure in the saddle, right up front. She thought she saw Ty off to the right of him. Another man rode forward and stopped next to Pa, and Edie didn't need him to move any closer to make out who he was.

James.

Her throat seemed to close up. He'd come in *with* her family. How had that happened? And all these men . . . She couldn't see who they were from here, but there could be only one explanation—they were from Crest Stone. And they'd volunteered to ride into this situation to rescue her.

If Edie hadn't been so fearful about what might happen next, she would've cried at the realization. Never, in her wildest dreams, could she have imagined so many people concerned for her life.

A few of the men dismounted—James, Pa, Ty. And as they moved forward, she made out Cousin Nick and Zeb too. The others remained in the saddle with guns drawn. The men on foot came closer and then stopped, just far enough away for Edie to make out the expressions on their faces—and to see that James's eyes were on her.

She tried to tell him everything with only her face, but that, of course, was impossible. What must he think of her? He had to know now. Did he figure it out on his own or did someone from her family tell him? And how had he found her family to begin with? He must be so angry with her.

But he'd come. With an army of men. And all of that despite the horrible memory of his own uncle riding into a similar situation. Edie chose to hold on to that fact and the sliver of hope that came with it. If she could do it all over again, she'd have told him the truth. Perhaps she could've prevented all of this from happening. And perhaps she would have lost him forever, but at least she'd be able to live with the knowledge that she'd done right.

If they both came out of this alive, she'd tell him everything.

"Virgil Fletcher." Pa's voice held an edge, yet it soothed Edie's soul. Leaving hadn't been an easy decision. As despicable as the things her father and brothers did were, she loved them with all her heart. She hadn't realized how much she'd missed her pa until he spoke. She wanted to slide out of Levi's grasp and run to him, let him keep her safe the way he always had.

"Jonas!" Virgil's voice was more gregarious. He opened his arms as if welcoming her family and all those men they rode in with to his home. "It's been a spell."

"We ain't here for a visit," Pa spat.

"Who's that with you?" Virgil continued, ignoring her father's impatience. "You have a bunch more kids?" And with that, he laughed. A few of his boys joined in.

"This here's James Wright, sheriff's deputy from up in Cañon City," Pa said. "And his men."

Next to him, James shifted, his hand resting on the handle of the revolver at his hip, but he said nothing. Instead, he seemed to keep close watch of each man before him.

"You brung the law into this?" Virgil said, his voice incredulous.

"You crossed the line when you took my daughter." Pa stood, his arms crossed.

"I'm only here to ensure this doesn't end in bloodshed," James said. "Now how about you call off those guns, Fletcher? Beaumont's here for talking, not shooting."

Virgil didn't reply right away. After a moment he motioned for the men to lower their weapons, but, Edie noticed, every one held tight to the gun at his side.

"What are your terms?" Pa asked, his eyes straying to Edie for the first time. She wished she could explain everything to him—how stifled and unhappy she'd been in Kansas, how different she felt in Crest Stone, and how badly she wanted a future that had nothing to do with living off ill-gotten money. But of course she couldn't. Instead, she was pinned beneath Levi's arm, helpless to do anything but watch as these men debated her release.

"We want the state," Virgil said.

Edie's heart sunk. Pa would never agree to that. Where would they go? Kansas was their home.

Pa's gaze snapped back to him. "The state," he repeated.

"I don't care where you go or what you do, but I want your family out of Kansas. For good."

Across from her, Edie's oldest brother, Ty, exchanged glances with Nick, who shook his head. Even James frowned. This was not going well . . .

Pa's expression was unreadable. "I got about forty men here who say otherwise."

At that, James turned his frown on Edie's pa. "We're not here to ensure you get what you want."

"And I got your girl," Virgil said. "You don't agree to my terms, I might be inclined to take her with us."

Edie stumbled as Levi turned her toward Virgil. Across from them, James's face took on a look Edie had never seen. His brow creased into an angry line and his expression grew hard.

"Or maybe I don't want the burden of riding a woman clear back to Kansas. We could end this now," Virgil said.

Behind her, Levi's heavy frame moved, and before Edie knew what was happening, he held a pistol in his left hand.

She gasped, and it felt as if her heart had lodged itself up into her throat. All she knew was that she needed to move, to run, to get away from here as fast as possible. The blood pounded in her ears, and she pushed against his arm, struggling to break free.

But Levi held firm. "You know I owe you for my leg, Beaumont," he said, his voice low and barely even. It was as if he struggled to contain something inside.

Out of breath, Edie stopped pushing against him. Trying to break free of this man was like attempting to move one of the mountains off to the west. Her eyes searched her pa, Ty, Zeb, Nick, and finally landed on James. His hand had closed around the handle of his revolver now, and his hard, practiced lawman's expression had disappeared. He scowled at Levi.

This had to end. Tempers ran too high, and Edie couldn't tell who was closest to being driven over the edge. If anyone died tonight because of her, she wouldn't be able to bear it. It had been her decision to come to Crest Stone, her decision to present herself as someone else, her decision to allow James's attentions, and her decision to ride out and attempt to find her family.

And now it would be her decision to stop all of this.

"Make your choice, Beaumont," Virgil was saying, looking off to the mountains as if he didn't have a care in the world. "Kansas or your lovely daughter."

James reached out and grabbed hold of Pa's arm the moment he began to take a step forward. Behind her, Levi tensed.

It was now or never.

"I have something better than some used up territory back in Kansas," she said, her voice sounding as if it was being raked over rocks.

All eyes moved to her, waiting, and she swallowed.

"Already told you I don't want your money, girl," Virgil said, his attention already straying back to the men before him.

"And that's not what I'm offering."

Across from her, James raised his eyebrows. She gave him only a moment, trying beyond hope to explain her plan with her eyes. She didn't dare look at him any longer. She drew in a deep breath and arranged her face to look as if she was offering the Fletchers the world. As if she wasn't in the least bit afraid of what might happen, despite the fact she could see Levi's revolver just out of the corner of her eye. "The Colorado & New Mexico is building an office in town to sell off the land it acquired around the railroad tracks. While it's under construction, they're keeping the deeds in the hotel safe."

"I ain't got much use for land," Virgil said. The wind rose as he stared at her, lifting the hems of Edie's skirts and sending the tendrils of hair that had fallen around her face flying.

"I don't propose you set up a ranch," Edie said, hoping she sounded as if she was in complete control, when in truth, her heart raced and it was a fight to keep from shrinking back into silence. "If you had these deeds in your possession, you could sell off that land and keep the money. And I can get them for you. A lot of men are itching to get their hands on some of those parcels," she added quickly.

It was all a lie. Edie didn't have the first clue where the railroad company kept its deeds, but she'd gotten Virgil's interest, at least. He seemed to be engaging in a silent conference with Levi and Whiskey Jack. Edie used that moment to glance off to her left. Pa saw right through her ruse, or so she assumed from the amused expression that crinkled around his eyes and lifted the corners of his lips while the Fletchers weren't looking. But James . . .

She hadn't prepared herself for his disappointment. He didn't know she was telling a falsehood, of course, and the hurt that had spread across his face hit her heart like an arrow.

He thought she was no better than the rest of her family.

Edie could have crumpled right there in the sage and sandy dirt, her hands still tied in front of her, and given up. James's disappointment in her was more than she could bear. But she forced herself to remain standing. If this worked, she could explain it to him. Perhaps he'd understand.

Or perhaps he was done with her the moment he found out who she really was.

"All right, you got my curiosity aroused, girl," Virgil said, and Edie swung all her attention back to the matter at hand. "But how do I know you're telling me the truth?"

"I have one of the deeds on me. I was going to give it to my pa, you see . . ." Edie fumbled for the pocket in her dress. She made quite a show of it, using her tied hands as an excuse.

"Pa, I didn't . . . I mean, I know I should have . . ." Tell stumbled over his words.

Edie knew exactly what he was trying to say. He hadn't bothered to find out whether she carried a small revolver or any other weapon, never mind a deed. He'd assumed correctly that she was unarmed, although he didn't know that.

Virgil's eyes shifted to his son. "Spit it out."

"I didn't—"

But before he could finish, Edie had dipped lower, grabbed two handfuls of sand and flung them behind her, right into Levi Fletcher's face.

Chapter Thirty-one

The moment Edie began fumbling for her pocket, James knew something wasn't right. He went from profoundly disappointed to confused to springing into action in less than five seconds.

As soon as Edie reached for the ground, James anticipated her actions. And the very second that sandy dirt hit Levi Fletcher in the face, he ran forward, guns drawn. Edie collided with him as she ran for safety, and he shoved her behind him just as the rest of Virgil's boys realized what was going on and began to fire. "Stay back!" he yelled at her over his shoulder.

This sort of melee was exactly the sort of thing James was hoping to avoid, but as the meeting drug on, he'd begun to think it was inevitable. Years of tensions had brewed between these two families, and they were long overdue to explode.

His only goal now was to make the violence last as short a time as possible. He went straight for Virgil, knowing Jonas Beaumont was likely to do the same. But James was younger and faster, and he was on Virgil before the man had even finished pulling his gun from his holster.

"Leave it be, Fletcher," he called, both guns trained on the man. He darted a look to either side, but Virgil's boys were too busy fighting off the Beaumonts and James's men to provide their father with any sort of protection. A few gunshots rang out here and there, but the Fletchers were severely outnumbered, and most of the men were quickly overpowered.

Virgil grinned, his eyes alight with some sort of madness, and he drew anyway. In a split second, James had to make a decision. He fired, praying the bullet would land where he intended it.

It did, and Virgil yelped, dropping the gun. James took a step forward, but stopped short when a voice rang through the mess of men and guns and fighting.

"Jonas Beaumont!"

James whipped around. Levi Fletcher, his vision seemingly clear of sand now, trained a revolver on Jonas Beaumont.

"Hold him!" James shouted at the nearest couple of men from town and pointed at Virgil Fletcher. The men did as they were told, and James moved toward the situation about to erupt between Levi and Jonas.

"Killing is too good for you," Levi was saying as Jonas backed up, both hands raised. "You crippled me, remember?" He spat the words out.

James paused just off to Levi's side. Around him, his men and the Beaumonts had mostly contained the Fletchers, but James kept his attention trained on Levi.

"Let's see how good you do on a bum leg." Levi lowered his revolver to aim at Jonas's leg.

James trained his own gun on Levi. "Let it go."

Levi offered him a mere glance before returning his attention to Jonas. "I'd like to see you stop me, lawman," he said. He placed both hands on the revolver.

And with Levi about to fire, James holstered his own gun before hurtling himself at Levi.

But he wasn't fast enough. Levi swung around and fired.

The impact should have knocked James backward, but he paused only a split second before continuing to move forward. He barreled into Levi, pushing the man to the ground, just as he began to feel the pain.

It exploded, so intense he thought he might black out.

James barely realized what was happening as two of his men held Levi to the ground. James backed away, stumbling, before falling to the ground.

"James!" Edie's voice reached his ears just as his eyes closed.

James opened his eyes to find an angel hovering over him. He lifted his hand to touch her face. She hardly looked real. But she frowned at him and gently pushed his hand down.

THEN SHE PRESSED FIRE to his other shoulder.

Jolted completely awake, the memories flooded back. The meetup, Edie tossing sand into Levi Fletcher's face, the Beaumonts and his men overtaking the Fletchers, and Levi Fletcher, shooting him.

And now Edie was . . . what *was* she doing?

He swatted at where she was inflicting so much pain he thought he might black out again. But she grabbed hold of his wrist and pulled his arm away. When had she gotten so strong?

Or, when had he become so weak?

"You need to let me tend to you," she said in an authoritative voice. He was reminded of a teacher he'd had in school back in Kansas, one who hadn't let him or any of the other boys get away with much of anything.

"You're lucky the bullet went clean through. But I have to clean the wound and stitch it up, or you'll lose the use of your entire arm."

His eyes found hers, and she looked down at him, deadly serious and yet so beautiful at the same time. Was there any end to what this woman could do? And yet something sat uneasy in his stomach . . . what was it?

She pressed fire to his shoulder again, and he realized, through the searing pain, that someone had cut away his shirt.

"All right," she said, more softly. "Mr. Johansen and Mr. Clements—they've been working on the bank—are going to hold your arms. I'll work as quickly as I can." She paused a moment, a hand hovering over his face. She finally let her fingers run quickly down his jaw, a feather-light touch he might've thought he'd imagined if he hadn't seen it happen. "I'm grateful you're alive." Her voice broke a little, but she recovered fast, backing away to allow the men from town to grab hold of his hands.

She took a needle and some thread from a younger man, a boy, really, who stood off to the side, and that was when the truth ricocheted back through him.

That boy was her brother.

Edie was a Beaumont.

And if that wasn't bad enough, she told lies as if they were truths, falling off her tongue as if the speaking of them was something that came easy to her.

James struggled, pushing against the men's grips. They mistook his movements for fear and held him tighter. Edie's needle pierced his skin, and James fought the urge to cry out.

"Here, give him this," someone said, and a piece of wood pressed between his teeth.

The torture went on for a few more minutes, until Edie had sewed up the holes on both the front and back of his shoulder.

"When we get back to town, I can make you a poultice that will help heal the wound," Edie said, but the last of her words trailed off, as if she weren't certain of them. Someone brought her a canteen to clean her hands while a couple of the men from town helped James up into a sitting position.

The pain was sharp, and he gritted his teeth until he could be still again. "The Fletchers," he managed to say as soon as he could think straight.

"All trussed up and ready to sit in jail," Clements said. He pinched the edges of his jacket between his fingers, looking awfully proud of himself.

James nodded, until the pain said otherwise. He sucked in a breath before speaking again. "Virgil Fletcher? How bad did I hit him?"

"Don't look like he's headed for the other side just yet. You grazed him good, though," Johansen said.

Edie finished washing her hands just as her father joined her. He immediately wrapped her into a hug. James wanted to smile at the affection, but something—something selfish and uncertain—wouldn't let him.

Clements and Johansen spoke of everything that had just happened, but James had eyes only for Edie. She spoke with her father for several minutes. At one point, he glanced at James with a slight frown before turning his attention back to his daughter. James couldn't imagine what she told him—or what he wanted her to tell him. He shouldn't still be thinking of her with affection, especially after everything she'd chosen not to share with him. And especially now that he knew who she was.

And yet . . . She had his heart.

With one last squeeze of her father's hand, Edie left him standing several feet away and stepped forward until she stood before James. "Excuse me, gentlemen," she said to Clements and Johansen. "Could I have a moment with Deputy Wright?"

The men tugged on their hats and walked off, leaving the two of them alone—or as alone as they could be with a large group of men all around them.

Edie knelt in the dirt beside him. "How does it feel?"

"It's painful, but not terrible," he said honestly. "Thank you for fixing me up."

She nodded, her cheeks coloring as she looked toward the ground. "I . . ." She glanced up toward where her father stood with a couple of men he presumed were her brothers. "My father would like to speak with you."

James pressed his lips together. He didn't have to talk with the man to know what he'd want—James's earlier promise to him fulfilled.

"Will you let them go free?" Edie's eyes were on him now, a soft brown, shining through the glasses that sat on her nose. Her voice was pleading, and it cut his heart in two.

By all that was just, he shouldn't. Yet . . . he'd made a promise, and he wasn't one to go back on his word. He had the Fletchers, and that was justice enough for his uncle. And in talking with Jonas Beaumont, he'd learned the crimes perpetrated had been the Fletchers, all save the horse thieving and the general store. The Fletchers had been the ones who'd ambushed him outside the mining camp.

"Yes," he said, a bit gruffly. "Provided they swear never to return."

She smiled at him, so big it seemed she'd pulled the sun down from the sky to light up her own face. And the last bit of reticence melted inside him. This woman meant the world to him, no matter her true name.

He loved her.

He wanted more than anything to take her hand in his and profess just that, but he couldn't—not yet.

"Thank you," she said as she twisted her hands together. Hands that had stitched him up. Hands that he'd held so recently he could place each detail of how they felt sitting in his own. "James, I . . ." Her mouth worked as if words were trying to escape, yet didn't quite know the way.

He wanted to ask her a million questions. Why did she keep the truth from him? Why didn't she come to him before she left? Did she care for him as much as he cared for her? But he kept his mouth shut, letting her figure out what she wanted to say.

"I owe you some explanation," she finally said. Her hands were clenched together now, and she sat still.

"You only need say what you feel you should," he replied. And he meant it. If she didn't care to tell him the truth, that was her decision. It might render his heart forever broken, but he'd have the answer to where her feelings lay. He'd move on, position himself as best he could to be elected town marshal, and finally achieve the life he'd wanted for so long.

Yet, why did it feel so hollow now?

"The truth is . . ." Edie paused, her eyes lifting to meet his, earnestness written all over her face. "I love you."

Chapter Thirty-two

The words hung in the air. James's eyes widened, and Edie was sure that if she gave it a moment, he'd speak, but she had more to say before he told her he couldn't feel the same way. The truth had been scratching at her insides for so long, and if she didn't let it out, she would never forgive herself.

She clasped her hands together so hard, her fingers began to tingle, and she pressed on. "I want you to know that. And I know you can't feel the same way, now that you're aware of who I am . . . who my family is. I wanted to tell you, so many times. And I almost did, but I couldn't bear the thought of hurting you. I thought it might be easier for both of us if I simply disappeared. But that didn't go as I planned, and while I was with the Fletchers, I promised myself that if I was afforded the opportunity, I'd tell you everything. You deserve the truth."

James opened his mouth to speak, but Edie didn't let him. "I left Kansas in the dead of night. I told no one. My family didn't know where I was, or even whether I was alive. I hated doing that to them, but it was the only way. My father never would have agreed, and I wanted out so badly. His life—and my mother's and my brothers'—it was never for me. All the stealing and sneaking around and constantly moving and always wondering whose lives lay in ruin because of my family . . . I couldn't live with that anymore. I wanted something stable and honest. I didn't want to be Edith Beaumont."

When she paused, James stayed quiet. Edie shifted herself, tucking her legs underneath her, and continued. "I took some money Mama had squirreled away, I wrote a false letter of reference, and I left. I'd seen an ad for waitresses, out here in the Colorado Territory. It felt far away, and so I took a train to Wichita and interviewed. I won the position, and . . ." She lifted an arm, gesturing to the landscape around them—the mountains on each side of the valley, the miles and miles of emptiness, the dark pines that dotted the landscape, and off in the distance, beyond where they could see, the new town of Crest Stone. "I love it here. I took an assumed name, I made friends, I worked hard."

"What about Mr. Adkins?" James finally spoke. His voice was kind but insistent.

Edie's heart tripped. The embarrassment of that entire incident was something she felt she'd never shed. "I should have told you, I know. But you must understand that was one of the worst experiences of my life. I didn't want you to look at me any differently, and all I wanted was to put it behind me. Mr. Adkins recognized me. He did work for my family in the past—and apparently the Fletchers too. He threatened to expose me if I didn't take money from the hotel for him. When we were found out, I told everyone that my family had owed him a debt, and that was what the money was for. He stayed quiet because I told him I'd already written my pa about what he'd done. It worked, until he decided it would be all right to write to the Fletchers and tell them about me. That's how they found me here."

James shifted his arm and winced. Edie reached out to check that the bandage was still in place, and he watched her work quietly. Finally, he spoke. "I understand. And I imagine anyone else would have done the same in your position."

"I suppose," she said, pulling her hand from his shoulder. The bandages held. Her only worry now was the possibility of infection setting in. But the poultice should help with that. They needed to return to town as soon as possible so she could make it. "But I doubt many others would have lied as I did. I was wrong to pretend I was someone I'm not. I thought it wouldn't affect anyone but myself, but it's hurt so many."

James looked as if he wanted to speak, but Edie stood quickly. She'd finally spoken aloud the thoughts that had troubled her for so long, and if she thought on them much longer, the guilt might tear her apart. Besides, she didn't think she could bear James's rejection. "We need to get moving." And with that, she turned to see if the rest of their party was ready.

Her pa stood off to the side, hand on his reliable old horse, and eyes that seemed to have been watching her this entire time. They hadn't said much earlier. Edie had apologized for leaving without a word, and he'd nodded gruffly before wrapping her in a hug. But that was all. She still felt as if there were so much more to say. She gathered her skirts and approached him.

"We need to return to Crest Stone as soon as possible. He needs rest or that wound won't heal properly," she said, with a glance back at James.

Her pa rubbed a hand across the back of his neck. "You've been awful attentive to the deputy."

Edie resisted the urge to wipe her damp palms across her skirts. "He was shot, and needed tending."

"You got your mother's ways of healing," he said with a sad smile. "But it ain't just that."

"What do you mean?" She spoke the words lightly, but her voice trembled just a little.

"For the love of Pete, girl, you're old enough to know your own mind. Do I have to spell it out for you?"

Edie glanced back at James. He watched her, his expression unreadable. "It doesn't matter," she said softly. "I've tangled myself in so many lies, he has no reason to trust me."

Pa's large hand squeezed her shoulder, immediately making her feel like a little girl again. As if all she had to do was curl up in her pa's embrace and all would be right with the world. She wanted to do that now. Throw herself into him and let him fix everything.

But he couldn't. Not this time.

"Edith. I can't say I much care for you taking up with a lawman, but if the man's heart is in the right place, he'll forgive you. And if it ain't, well . . . I don't like him anyways."

"Because he's a lawman?"

"I like staying alive." With that he winked at her. "I'm not going back to town with you. The boys and I are going to head out, back to Kansas, where we belong. We could wait . . ."

Edie shut her eyes. If James rejected her, would she want to return home? Seeing her family again was wonderful, but she knew, deep down, she'd never be happy there. The reason she left still remained. "No, you don't need to. If things . . . well, I always have my work at the hotel." Provided she still had a position there after all of this, which was doubtful.

"All right, then. I'll give your mother your love."

"I'd like that, Pa. Thank you." Edie's eyes filled with tears, and she blinked them away as Pa ruffled the mess of her hair.

"Zeb, Ty. Help that lawman get on his horse." Pa motioned to Edie's brothers as he crossed the short distance to speak with James.

And before she knew it, they were on their way back to Crest Stone.

Chapter Thirty-three

Days had passed since Edie was found. Her poultice had helped his wound begin to close up, and James began to wonder if there was anything she couldn't heal. Accompanied by volunteers from town, he'd escorted the Fletchers to the jail in Cañon City. Sheriff Young was happy with his work, and James had returned to Crest Stone, relieved to have the Fletchers behind bars and the Beaumonts on their way back to Kansas. Yet he still felt uneasy.

Edie was never far from his mind. He'd seen her a couple of times at the hotel. They'd spoken, but only of inconsequential things. And while she'd smiled at him, there was something sad and hollow in her eyes. It was a look that made him want to take her up in his arms, kiss her, and tell her nothing would ever hurt her again. But he'd resisted, all because of that little voice in the back of his head that reminded him of how much she'd kept from him.

Antsy one afternoon after making his rounds of town, James found himself strolling down the old wagon path to the creek behind the hotel. He didn't know where he was going or why he'd chosen this path, but he felt the need to keep moving. There was something that had been bothering him, something just out of reach, and maybe if he kept going, he'd figure it out.

It was Edie, of course. Everything in his head lately was Edie. But it was something she'd said. Or maybe it was something she hadn't said, back at the old cabin. But what was it?

He kept to the creek bank as the water roared south. The spring melt had come down from the mountains fast this year. The water made him think of his own mind, running miles in barely a minute. He paused and took in the water, so certain about where it was heading. He was looking at it differently, seeing it in a way he hadn't before . . .

That was it.

James squatted by the bank and pulled off a glove to dip his fingers into the crystal-clear water. The cold of it bit at his skin and cleared his mind. And when he stood, it was all there.

Edie hadn't told him the truth because she was afraid he would see her differently.

He'd told her about his uncle's death, but hadn't been entirely honest about what it had done to him—because he didn't want her to see him differently. As a weak man, or as someone afraid of love. But he was afraid of it. In fact, the very thought of trusting anyone that much scared him to death.

He spun on his heel there on the muddy bank and walked with purpose back toward the hotel. He needed to find her, to talk to her. He rounded the trees that marked the start of the wagon path and stopped short.

It couldn't be, but it was.

Right in front of him was Edie, wearing a simple blue gingham dress and carrying a glass jar. She paused when she saw him, smiling at first, and then, almost as if she'd caught herself, letting that sad look take over her face.

He'd do anything to keep her from looking that way ever again.

"Edie?" he said hesitantly.

"I'm sorry. I thought I might look for some wild herbs and flowers down here. But I can go—"

"No." He took three steps forward until he was right in front of her.

She took a tiny step backward, her eyes darting around him. "I . . ."

"Please. I want to speak with you."

She stopped, the jar clutched between her hands. "I lost my position. I'm not certain if you knew."

The sorrow in her words felt as if it had invaded James's heart. "I'm so sorry."

"I knew word would reach the McFarlands or Mrs. Ruby, so I told them myself. About how I'd created a new name for myself and a false letter of reference to obtain work at the hotel. It might damage the reputation of the hotel if they let me stay on, so . . . " She looked down at her jar, and the sunlight through the trees dappled the strands of her hair. "They've been nothing but kind to me, though. Mr. McFarland said I can remain here until I can ascertain my next step."

"They're good people."

Edie glanced through the trees behind her, toward the hotel that was hidden from view. "I'll miss my work there. I . . . I'm not certain where to go from here, or what to do. I don't know that I have it in me to pretend to be someone else all over again." Unshed tears filled her eyes, and she blinked them away.

He ought to ask her what her plans were, but he didn't want to hear. Not yet. Not until he'd told her everything. If she wanted to break his heart then, at least he'd have been honest to her about his own feelings. He took in a deep breath, trying to figure out how to articulate all the thoughts in his head. "*I don't want you to be anyone else. I don't see you any differently. Yes, I know your real name now, and I know what you did to get here and how you had to deal with Mr. Adkins. But I still see *you*."

"You see me," she said, echoing his words with confusion lacing her voice.

"No matter what you call yourself, you're still a woman of courage. One who didn't fear starting a new life, alone in a place like this. A woman who isn't afraid to love things that are a little out of the ordinary—herbs and medicines, books about plants. A woman who didn't care a whit about what anyone else might think when you came to my room to ensure I had enough of your tea to see me through the next day."

She blinked at him like a deer who'd spotted a hunter.

"Don't you see?" He took her hand. "It doesn't matter that you kept those secrets when you were honest about your true self. And I . . . Well, I haven't been exactly honest either."

She raised her eyes from their joined hands. "What do you mean?"

"I told you about my uncle and about why I wanted to be a lawman. But I never told you what his death did to me. It scared me so much that I didn't believe I could trust how I felt about you. In my mind, falling in love meant losing my focus. It meant certain death."

"Falling in love?" Her big brown eyes stared at him from behind her glasses.

"Yes. I'm in love with a woman who left everything she had to start a new, better life. A woman I know I can trust, because she hasn't wavered." He paused a moment, letting his words catch up with everything that ran through his head. "I love you, Edie."

A small tear formed at the corner of her eye. He lifted his other hand to wipe it away, and she smiled tentatively at him.

"I love you too. I thought . . . I thought you didn't want me. And I understood why. But oh, James, I promise to never keep secrets again. It tore me apart each day, seeing you and laughing with you and yet fearing what you'd think if you knew where I'd come from."

He let his hand drift to her cheek. Her skin was so soft, and when she leaned her face into his touch, he thought he might burst from the need to kiss her. "Edith Beaumont, will you marry me?"

She laughed as more tears found their way from her eyes. "Yes, I will. I absolutely will."

And with that, he pulled her to him, letting his other arm wrap around her shoulders as his mouth found hers. She melted into him, and he thought he might never leave this very spot. Her jar dropped to the ground as she held him close. Edie was warmth and happiness and comfort. She was his future.

And together, they'd have nothing to fear.

Epilogue

Early June was a wonder to behold in the valley. Edie would never grow tired of the brightness of the grasses, the softer green of the sagebrush, the blue of the sky, the white snow that still sat on the mountaintops in the distance, and now, the earthy brown of the wood that was the beginnings of the construction of their new home.

She bit her lip to keep from laughing. She laughed more now, she'd begun to notice. Maybe it was because she felt so light, so much more free without the burden of her past tugging her down. So many people knew now who she was. But it didn't matter. Since announcing her engagement to James, Edie felt more at peace with herself. It was freeing, no longer fearing someone finding out about her family and no longer needing to keep up the pretense she had for months. James knew, and he loved her as she was, and that was all that mattered.

"We'll have four rooms," James said to her as he approached after speaking with the men who were helping to build the house. "A parlor and a kitchen, and two bedrooms."

Edie smiled, thinking of the children she hoped they'd have to fill that second bedroom. "It'll be perfect." She turned to look at the man who would, in a week's time, be her husband. The small church wasn't completely built yet, so they'd made plans to travel to Cañon City for the ceremony.

But today, James had work to do.

"When do you suppose you'll return?" Edie asked as he wrapped his arms around her. She'd never grow tired of this. She placed her hands on his chest so she could look up and see his face.

"Tomorrow, most likely. It's a long ride south." He grinned at her as if he weren't about to embark on a journey to search for a dangerous gang of train robbers.

"I'm glad you aren't going alone." Some of the same men who'd helped him find her volunteered to help James with this search.

"Why, Edie, are you afraid something might happen to me?" He nuzzled her nose with his, and she laughed.

"I'm *always* afraid something might happen to you. Be careful, please."

He dropped his smile. "I will, I promise. We aren't certain who these men are, but it appears to be a different group than the one that hit the train north of here in April."

She traced one of the buttons on his vest. "Just come back to me. That's all I want."

"I'd love to see anyone try to stop me from doing that."

When she looked back up at him, his eyes held an intensity she'd seen only a few times. It took her breath away, the way he looked at her like she was the only other person who existed in the world. It made her legs feel as if they might buckle beneath her. He caught her lips with his, and her mind ceased to function. All she could do was let her arms wrap around him, and lose herself entirely.

He backed away for just a moment, long enough to say, "I'll always come back to you." And then his mouth was on hers again, her eyes fluttered shut, and she knew one thing for certain.

No one could ever see her the way James did.

THANK YOU FOR READING! I hope you enjoyed James and Edie's story! Now you'll have to find out what happens when Dora starts her mail-order bride business in the brand new Crest Stone Mail-Order Brides series. Will brokenhearted Clara find happiness with Roman, the cowboy-turned-livery owner? Find out in *A Hopeful Bride*[1].

I owe a debt of gratitude to those who helped me name the Fletchers. Thank you *so* much to Janet Simmons, Rose Hale, Arletta Boulton, and Johnna Darbonne. Your names helped shape these characters' personalities, and I'm ever grateful to you!

---

1. *https://bit.ly/HopefulBride*

To be alerted about new books, sign up here: http://bit.ly/catsnewsletter I give subscribers a free download of *Forbidden Forever*, a Gilbert Girls prequel novella (it tells the story of Mr. and Mrs. McFarland). You'll also get sneak peeks at upcoming books, insights into the writer life, discounts and deals, inspirations, and so much more. I'd love to have *you* join the fun!

Turn the page to see a complete list of the books in the Gilbert Girls series, along with the other books I've written.

More Books by Cat Cahill

Books in *The Gilbert Girls* series
Building Forever[1]
Running From Forever[2]
Wild Forever[3]
Hidden Forever[4]
Forever Christmas[5]
On the Edge of Forever[6]
The Gilbert Girls Book Collection – Books 1-3[7]
***Crest Stone Mail-Order Brides* series**
A Hopeful Bride[8]
A Rancher's Bride[9]
***Brides of Fremont County* series**
Grace[10]
Molly[11]
Other Sweet Historical Western Romances by Cat
***The Proxy Brides* series**

---

1. http://bit.ly/BuildingForeverbook

2. http://bit.ly/RunningForeverBook

3. http://bit.ly/WildForeverBook

4. http://bit.ly/HiddenForeverBook

5. http://bit.ly/ForeverChristmasBook

6. http://bit.ly/EdgeofForever

7. http://bit.ly/GilbertGirlsBox

8. https://bit.ly/HopefulBride

9. http://bit.ly/RanchersBride

10. http://bit.ly/ConfusedColorado

11. https://bit.ly/DejectedDenver

A Bride for Isaac [12]
A Bride for Andrew [13]
A Bride for Weston[14]
***The Blizzard Brides* series**
A Groom for Celia [15]
***The Matchmaker's Ball* series**
Waltzing with Willa[16]

12. http://bit.ly/BrideforIsaac

13. https://bit.ly/BrideforAndrew

14. https://bit.ly/BrideforWeston

15. http://bit.ly/GroomforCelia

16. https://bit.ly/WaltzingwithWilla

About the Author, Cat Cahill

A sunset. Snow on the mountains. A roaring river in the spring. A man and a woman who can't fight the love that pulls them together. The danger and uncertainty of life in the Old West. This is what inspires me to write. I hope you find an escape in my books!

I live with my family, my hound dog, and a few cats in Kentucky. When I'm not writing, I'm losing myself in a good book, planning my next travel adventure, doing a puzzle, attempting to garden, or wrangling my kids.

Made in United States
Troutdale, OR
02/17/2024

17766222R00098